INTRODUCTION TO CHEMISTRY

Jane Chisholm and Mary Johnson
Consultant editor: Alan Alder
Designed by Iain Ashman

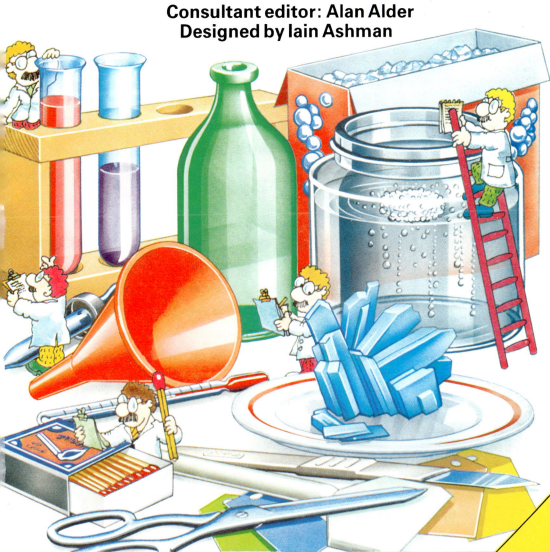

Illustrated by Jeremy Banks, Sue Stitt, Chris Lyon, Jeremy Gower, Graham Smith, Graham Round, Simon Roulstone and Penny Simon

Computer program by Chris Oxlade

WITH COMPUTER PROGRAM LISTING

Contents

- 3 What is chemistry?
- 5 Looking at chemicals
- 6 What things are made of
- 8 Looking at particles
- 10 Physical changes
- 12 What is a chemical reaction?
- 14 Looking for patterns in chemistry
- 16 Why chemical reactions happen
- 18 Understanding compounds
- 21 Valencies
- 22 Fast and slow reactions
- 24 Catalysts
- 26 How metals react
- 28 Acids, bases and salts
- 30 What is organic chemistry?
- 32 Organic families
- 34 Useful organic compounds
- 36 Splitting compounds
- 38 Identifying substances
- 40 Computer program
- 42 Formulae and equations
- 44 Doing experiments
- 45 Answers to puzzles
- 46 Chemistry words
- 47 Useful information
- 48 Index

About this book

This book is a general introduction to the basic ideas of chemistry. It begins by looking at atoms and molecules and some of the ideas that chemistry is based on. This will help you understand what is going on in chemical reactions and why.

There are lots of experiments for you to try out if you want to. Don't worry if you find an experiment doesn't work first time. This can often happen, even to very experienced chemists. There are a lot of reasons why an experiment might go wrong – just try again. On page 44, there are tips on safety, and on getting the best results from your experiments. There's advice too about where to get hold of chemicals and other equipment.

At the back of the book, you can find the answers to puzzles and questions. There are also definitions of difficult or unfamiliar words, as well as useful charts and summaries. Chemists write down chemical reactions in "formulae" and "equations". You can find out about writing equations at the back too.

If you have a home computer, or can borrow one from someone, there's a program to try out. It helps you to identify unknown chemicals and is written to work on most common makes of home computer.

First published in 1983 by Usborne Publishing Ltd, 20 Garrick Street, London WC2E 9BJ, England
Copyright © 1983 Usborne Publishing
The name Usborne and the device ⛃ are Trade Marks of Usborne Publishing Ltd. All rights reserved. No part of this publication may be reproduced, stored in a retrieval system or transmitted in any form or by any means, electronic, mechanical, photocopying, recording or otherwise, without the prior permission of the publisher.

Printed by
Graficas Reunidas SA,
Madrid, Spain.

What is chemistry?

Chemistry is the study of chemicals. Everything around you is made of chemicals – the land, sea, sky, houses, cars, food, clothes and even your body.

There are just over a hundred basic chemicals. These are called elements. You will have heard of some of them already, such as gold or oxygen. Elements are the building bricks of chemistry. Although they can exist on their own, they are usually combined with other elements.

By studying what things are made of, and how they react with other things, chemists can work out how to make new, useful substances. Here are some of the things that chemists have invented.

Chemicals in laboratories may not seem very interesting, but, put together with other chemicals, they can produce all kinds of reactions – bangs, whizzes, flashes – and new chemicals are formed.

There are chemical reactions going on all around you – when you do the washing up, or strike a match, or cook something.

Medicines

Plastics

Nylon, acrylic, polyester, terylene, rayon and other artificial fibres.

Petrol

Paints, glues, dyes, cosmetics and household cleaners.

Fertilizers

Rust and buildings, blackened and worn away with age, are signs of chemical reactions too.

Your body is a bit like a large, rubbery test tube, with lots of chemical reactions going on inside. You add more chemicals – food and oxygen from the air – to keep all these reactions going.

How chemistry began

Chemistry comes from the Arabic, *al quemia*, meaning alchemy. Alchemy was an early form of chemistry, which began about 2,000 years ago. Alchemists began by trying to turn ordinary metals into gold. There was often a lot of magic and superstition involved. Alchemy was not a real science, although some scientific methods were used. They made some important discoveries, such as how to make medicines and drugs from herbs.

Modern chemistry probably began in the 17th century, when Robert Boyle defined elements. Another important step came in 1808, with John Dalton's atomic theory. He said that elements could be divided into tiny particles, called atoms. Ideas such as these provide the framework for modern chemistry.

How chemists work

A lot of science involves using ideas that have not yet been proved. So a chemist works a bit like a detective. In order to explain something, a chemist first makes an intelligent guess, called a hypothesis. The hypothesis is followed up by investigation. Lots of experiments are done and observations made. If the experiments all give the same answer, the hypothesis becomes a theory. If, over many years, it is never proved wrong, it becomes a natural law.

Chemistry involves studying tiny, but complicated particles. To describe them, chemists use simplified diagrams, like this one of an atom. No-one pretends that atoms actually look like this, but it shows the parts the chemist is interested in.

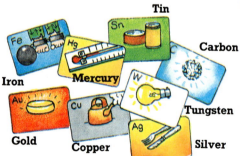

Chemists have developed their own language, which is understood all over the world. It involves writing in "formulae". Each element has a symbol, consisting of one or two letters. You can guess some of them, because they start with the first letter of the element's name (sometimes its Latin or Greek name).

Chemistry experiments can easily go wrong unless they are done very carefully. This is why chemists work in laboratories. There they can control the temperature, weigh things on very accurate scales, and keep the chemicals pure in airtight, glass containers.

Looking at chemicals

Chemists try to sort everything into groups, in order to make their work easier. There are lots of different ways of classifying chemicals. You can divide them into solids, liquids and gases, or into metals and non-metals. If you want to classify something, you can start by looking at its physical characteristics – or "properties", as chemists call them. Here are the sorts of questions that a chemist would ask.

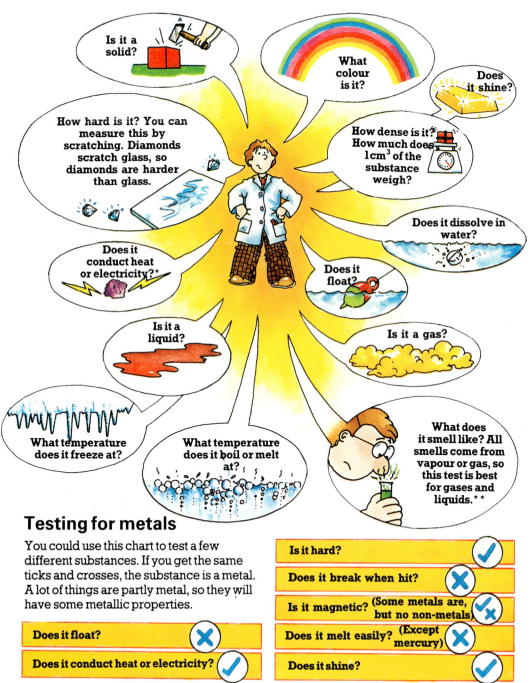

- Is it a solid?
- What colour is it?
- Does it shine?
- How hard is it? You can measure this by scratching. Diamonds scratch glass, so diamonds are harder than glass.
- How dense is it? How much does 1cm³ of the substance weigh?
- Does it dissolve in water?
- Does it conduct heat or electricity?*
- Does it float?
- Is it a liquid?
- Is it a gas?
- What temperature does it freeze at?
- What temperature does it boil or melt at?
- What does it smell like? All smells come from vapour or gas, so this test is best for gases and liquids.**

Testing for metals

You could use this chart to test a few different substances. If you get the same ticks and crosses, the substance is a metal. A lot of things are partly metal, so they will have some metallic properties.

Question	
Does it float?	✗
Does it conduct heat or electricity?	✓
Is it hard?	✓
Does it break when hit?	✗
Is it magnetic? (Some metals are, but no non-metals)	✓/✗
Does it melt easily? (Except mercury)	✗
Does it shine?	✓

*You can find out how to test this on page 18.
**Be careful! It's dangerous to get too close to a lot of chemicals.

What things are made of

Scientists believe that absolutely everything is made of particles. Imagine a piece of an element, such as copper. If it were possible to go on cutting it into smaller and smaller pieces, you would eventually get a tiny particle called an atom. An atom is the smallest particle that can exist and still have the properties of a particular element. The word comes from the Greek, *atomos*, meaning "indivisible". We can't see atoms properly, but knowing about them will help you understand chemical reactions better.

This is part of the tip of a needle, magnified about three million times. It is seen through a very powerful machine called a field-ion microscope. Each spot of light represents an atom.

Inside an atom

Each atom is a bit like a miniature solar system, with a nucleus in the middle and particles called electrons orbiting around outside it. All the atoms of an element are different from the atoms of other elements, and have different numbers of electrons. Atoms have lots of other particles too, but many of these have only recently been discovered and scientists don't yet know as much about them.

Electrons are particles with a negative electric charge. They travel round the nucleus in orbits.

2 Each atom of an element has a certain number of electrons. This is called its atomic number.

3 The electrons of an atom are arranged in different layers, or orbits. You can find out more about these on page 16.

4 Chemists believe that electrons usually spin in pairs. One goes clockwise, the other, anti-clockwise.

5 Chemists used to think that electrons moved in fixed orbits, like planets. They now believe that electrons can be anywhere within their orbit, at any time. Sometimes they may even be outside it. However, this would be very difficult to draw, so electron orbits are usually shown like this.

6 Atoms of different elements have a different size and weight. Chemists call this their "mass". We cannot weigh atoms, but we can work out their mass in comparison with other atoms. This is called the relative atomic mass. It is based on an atom of carbon, which is said to have a mass of 12.

*Plural of nucleus.

Radioactivity

Since the beginning of this century, scientists have known that atoms could be split. The nucleus of an atom contains a great deal of energy. Some isotopes of certain atoms have unstable nuclei,* which may fall apart giving off energy and radiation. They are called radioactive isotopes.

Atoms can be split artificially too. The energy can be trapped and used to provide light and heat. This is what nuclear power stations do. However this radiation, although invisible, is extremely dangerous. It is the basis of nuclear weapons.

Ordinary atoms go on forever, but radioactive ones have a fixed life-span. This can be seconds, or millions of years. Carbon 14** is slightly radioactive and disintegrates very slowly. It is used to work out the age of archaeological finds.

10 Usually all the atoms of an element have the same mass number, but some do not. These are called the different isotopes of an element.

9 The number of protons and neutrons added together is called the mass number of an atom

Most of an atom consists of empty space. Image the nucleus as the size of a pea in a international football pitch. Some of the electrons would be orbiting at the very edge of the stadium.

8 The nucleus also contains a number of uncharged, neutral particles, called neutrons.

11 Atoms are held together by the strong attraction between the protons and electrons. Particles with opposite charges attract one another, like opposite poles of a magnet.

7 The nucleus contains particles called protons, which have a positive electric charge. Atoms have the same number of protons as electrons. This makes them electrically neutral. Protons are about 1,860 times heavier than electrons.

**This means it has a mass number of 14, instead of 12, which most carbon atoms have

Looking at particles

Looking at how atoms behave can help you understand more about chemical reactions. Atoms rarely exist on their own. They usually group together in particles called molecules, or in giant structures called lattices.

A molecule is the smallest particle of a substance that can normally exist by itself. Hydrogen and oxygen atoms, for example, go around in pairs. So a molecule of hydrogen contains two atoms. Chemists write this as H_2, to show that there are two atoms.

Other molecules are made up of larger numbers of atoms. For example, phosphorus molecules contain four atoms. Sulphur molecules contain eight atoms in a ring.

Molecules of compounds contain different types of atoms bonded together in fixed proportions. Here are the molecules of a few different compounds. Their formulae show you how many atoms of each element there are in the molecule.

Solids, liquids and gases

Chemists call solids, liquids and gases the three states of matter. Any substance can change from one state to another, depending on its temperature and pressure. The difference between these states lies in how much the particles in the substance are moving around and how tightly packed together they are.

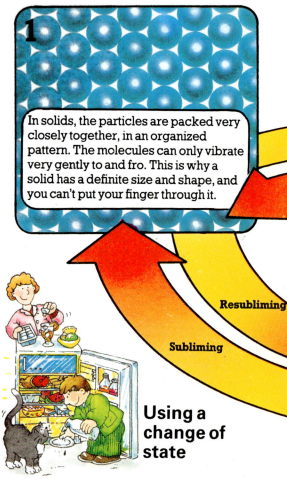

In solids, the particles are packed very closely together, in an organized pattern. The molecules can only vibrate very gently to and fro. This is why a solid has a definite size and shape, and you can't put your finger through it.

Using a change of state

Inside the back of a fridge is a liquid which boils and turns into a gas at a very low temperature. But in order to do this, it needs energy. It gets this energy by taking heat away from the inside of the fridge. As it does so, the fridge becomes much colder than the rest of the room. This keeps the food cool. At the back of the fridge is a "condenser", where the gas changes back into a liquid. As it does this, heat is given out from the back of the fridge. Put your hand there and feel how warm it is.

2

When particles are close together, they attract one another. So a lot of energy is needed to push them apart. Heat is a form of energy. When you heat a solid, it gives the particles energy. They start vibrating a lot and move away from each other. This is why things melt when you heat them. Chemists call this a change of state.

Changes of state

When something changes state, heat is always produced or lost. As water gets colder, it freezes into a solid – ice. If you heat it, it turns into a gas – water vapour. Your breath contains water vapour. If you breathe onto a very cold window pane, the cold will change the vapour back into tiny drops of water.

Melting

Freezing/Solidifying

3

The particles in a liquid are further apart than in a solid, but are still able to attract one another. They are not arranged in a regular pattern, and have no shape of their own. You can mould them to any shape you want, by putting them in a container.

You can break up the particles of a liquid or gas more easily than you can those of a solid, because of the spaces in between.

Condensing

Evaporating/Boiling

4

If you heat a liquid, the particles are given even more energy. They move around so much that they eventually escape from the surface of the liquid, and become a gas. The particles in a gas are moving around very fast, and cannot attract one another much. This is why a gas has no particular shape. It fills whatever space you put it in.

Why do you think a saucepan overflows when it is boiling?

Physical changes

When you mix two substances, their particles become jumbled up together. But they do not necessarily combine chemically. Unless the atoms in the molecules are rearranged, the change is only a physical one. The new substance is called a mixture and can usually be separated quite easily.

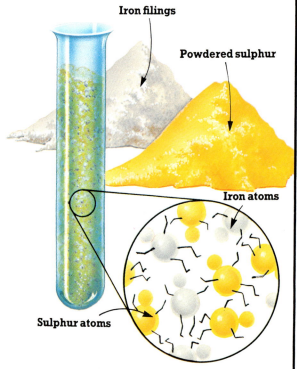

Iron filings

Powdered sulphur

Iron atoms

Sulphur atoms

The properties of substances in a mixture stay the same after they have been mixed. So you can use their properties to try to separate them. Try mixing together iron filings and powdered sulphur. Iron is a grey metal that sinks in water and is magnetic. Sulphur is a yellow non-metal that floats in water and is not magnetic. Can you think how to separate them? Try out your ideas to see if they work.

Separating puzzle

How would you separate these things? Tea and sugar, salt and flour, talc and bath salts, a broken jar of pins, a broken bottle of bath salts. Read these two pages first, for clues about which methods to use.

Separating things

A lot of chemicals are mixtures of things. If a chemist wants to analyse a substance, the first step is to break it down into elements and compounds. Here are some different ways of separating mixtures. If you know something about the physical properties of the ingredients, it will help you decide which method to use.

A solid dissolved in a liquid is called a solution. You can separate a solution by boiling it or leaving it to evaporate. Lemon juice is a mixture of things, including citric acid and water. To get rid of the water, boil it first, then leave it to evaporate. You will be left with solid crystals.

Lemons

Some metals are magnetic. You can separate them from other substances by using a magnet.

Magnet

An insoluble solid in a liquid is called a suspension. It should separate after being left to stand for a long time. The solid will settle at the bottom.

If a mixture contains an insoluble solid and a soluble one, you can separate them by adding water and then pouring it through filter paper. This method can be used to clean up dirty salt. Dissolve the mixture and filter off the dirt. To get back the salt, boil* off most of the water and leave the last bit to evaporate.

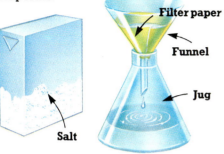

Distillation is a way of separating two liquids which have different boiling points. This is used in the manufacture of spirits, such as whisky. Alcohol boils at a lower temperature than water. The mixture is boiled and the alcohol vapour is collected in a test tube, then cooled back into a liquid. Separating it from some of the water makes the alcohol more concentrated. This is why spirits are stronger than beer and wine, which are not distilled.

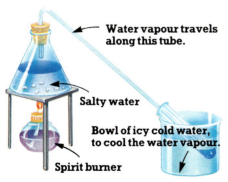

You can use this method to purify salty water. When the water changes into water vapour, it leaves behind the salt and other impurities. The vapour is then cooled to make pure, distilled water.

You can separate the chemicals in inks by a method called chromatography. Take a large piece of blotting paper, filter paper or kitchen towel and put some spots of coloured ink along the bottom. Hang this over a bowl of water, so that the paper just touches the water. As the water is soaked up, it carries the ink with it. Coloured fringes appear as different chemicals in the ink move different distances. This shows you that many inks are made up of different coloured chemicals.

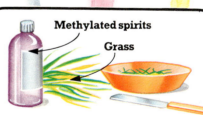

You can try separating the colours in grass. Chop up some bits of fresh grass in a bowl and crush them with a few drops of methylated spirits. Then do the same test, using methylated spirits instead of water.

11

*Take care not to boil the pan dry or you may ruin it.

What is a chemical reaction?

A chemical reaction is when a chemical change takes place and the atoms themselves are rearranged. This results in a new substance, or substances, being formed. The atoms in a molecule are bonded chemically. When a new compound is formed, these bonds are broken and the atoms regroup themselves. The atoms in a molecule are held together by strong bonds. This makes a compound difficult to split.

What makes a chemical reaction take place?

When a chemical reaction takes place, energy is usually absorbed or given off. Energy, in the form of heat, is often needed to start a reaction. This is why there are a lot of chemical reactions in cooking.

Unlike mixtures, compounds have different properties from those of the elements they contain. For example, sodium and chlorine are both very dangerous. But they combine to make sodium chloride, which is the salt you eat.

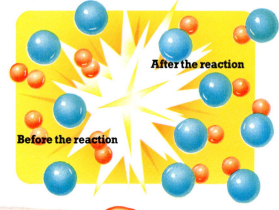

Is a cake a chemical reaction?

If you mix together butter, sugar, flour and baking powder, you get a mixture which still looks, tastes and feels like its ingredients. But when water is added and it is cooked you can see that a chemical reaction has taken place. The baking powder reacts with the other ingredients to give off bubbles of gas (carbon dioxide), which makes the mixture rise. The new substance looks, feels and tastes different from the uncooked mixture and cannot be separated back into the original ingredients.

These bubbles are made by carbon dioxide gas.

When you make a cake, it is important to get the quantities right, or the cake may not rise. It is just the same in other chemical reactions. Unlike mixtures, compounds contain ingredients in fixed proportions.

*You can find out about writing equations on page 42.

Chemical reactions in your body

The chemical reactions in your body also need energy. They use energy which is produced from eating food and breathing in oxygen. The food and oxygen react together to make water and energy, which you use, and carbon dioxide which you breathe out. You can write this in a word equation.

Carbohydrates + oxygen → water + carbon dioxide + energy

Make a compound

See if you can make a compound from the iron and sulphur mixture you made on page 10. Not all mixtures are capable of forming compounds.

Mix together six measures of iron to four measures of sulphur and heat them in a test tube. The tube should glow red* and leave a solid lump. This is the compound, iron sulphide.

Iron and sulphur

Tongs

Another test you can do is to put it in some acid. Iron sulphide should produce a gas with a "bad egg" smell.

Iron sulphide

Iron sulphide – gas with "bad egg" smell.

The compound formed is non-magnetic and sinks in water. So it doesn't behave like iron or sulphur. This is why it is difficult to separate.

Sulphur and acid – no reaction

Iron and acid – bubbles, but no smell.

Reactions which produce heat

You don't always need heat to set off a chemical reaction. Some reactions produce heat. Try mixing vinegar with bicarbonate of soda. Test the ingredients with a thermometer before and after the reaction. You should see a slight rise in temperature.

Reactions which use light

Plants use light energy, as well as heat, to carry out chemical reactions inside themselves. Compare this equation with the one for reactions inside your body. It's almost the same reaction in reverse.

Carbon dioxide + water → sugar + oxygen

*Take care! See page 44 for notes on safety.

Looking for patterns in chemistry

For centuries chemists have tried to sort chemistry into some sort of order, so as to understand it better. The first step was to identify the building bricks – the elements. By the 19th century, chemists were beginning to find patterns in the behaviour of elements. They found that some reacted often; others hardly at all. By doing lots of experiments they worked out that the atoms of different elements must have different "atomic weights".

A German chemist, Döbereiner, found that bromine, chlorine and iodine reacted similarly. He spotted several other groups and concluded that elements * could be grouped in threes, called triads. An English chemist, Newlands, came closer to the answer. He arranged the elements in order of atomic weight and noticed that elements with similar properties occurred at intervals of eight, which he called "octaves".

The Periodic Table

In 1869, a Russian chemist, Mendeleev, published his Periodic Table. He also arranged the elements in order of atomic weight, but leaving gaps for elements he believed had not yet been discovered. This system worked. As new elements have been found over the years, the gaps have been filled. This table can give you all kinds of clues about why particular elements behave as they do. You will find it useful to refer to as you read through the book.

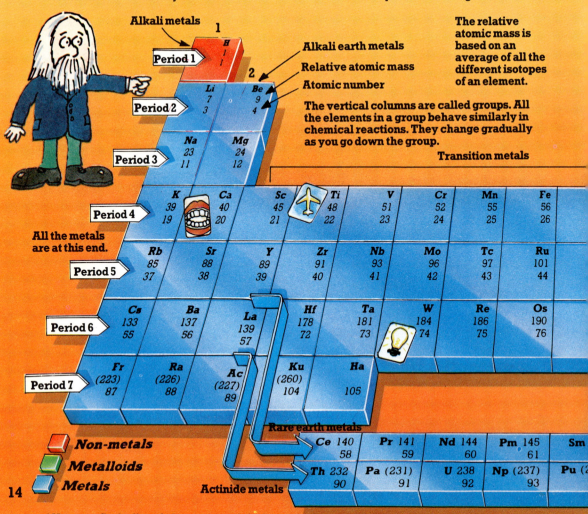

*You can find a list of elements and their symbols on page 47.

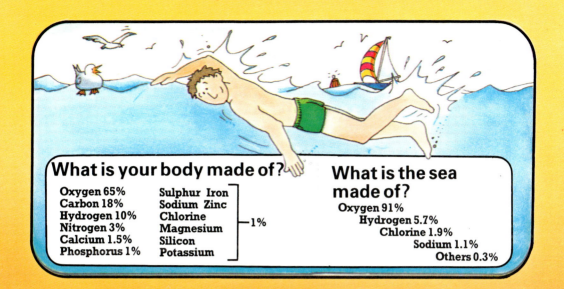
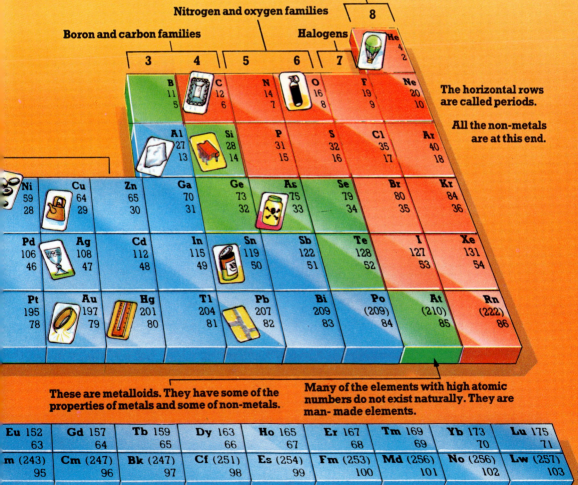

Why chemical reactions happen

Looking at an atom's structure can give you clues as to how it will react with other atoms. Scientists believe that the electrons in an atom are arranged in layers, called orbits. There's a limit to the number of electrons that can fit into each orbit. Atoms can have between one and seven orbits. In the Periodic Table, all the elements in a period usually have the same number of orbits. In period 1, they have one orbit, in period 2, they have two orbits, and so on...

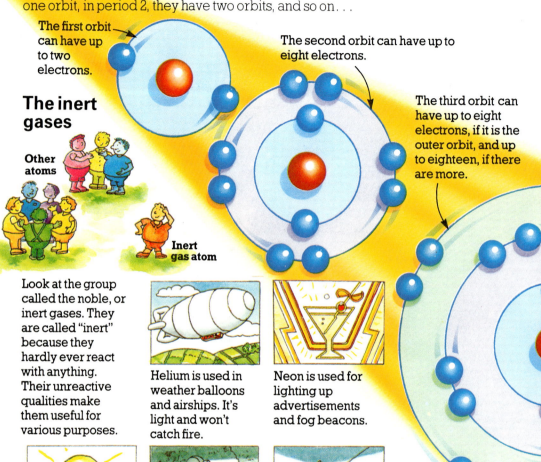

The first orbit can have up to two electrons.

The second orbit can have up to eight electrons.

The third orbit can have up to eight electrons, if it is the outer orbit, and up to eighteen, if there are more.

The inert gases

Other atoms

Inert gas atom

Look at the group called the noble, or inert gases. They are called "inert" because they hardly ever react with anything. Their unreactive qualities make them useful for various purposes.

Helium is used in weather balloons and airships. It's light and won't catch fire.

Neon is used for lighting up advertisements and fog beacons.

Argon

Krypton

Xenon

Argon is used in electric light bulbs. Krypton and xenon are used in special bulbs, such as those used in miners' lamps and in lighthouses. Radon is radioactive. It can be used to trace gas leaks and in treating some forms of cancer.

Why are the inert gases so unreactive?

Why do you think the inert gases are so unreactive? If you look at their structures, you will see that they all have full orbits. That is the clue. Atoms like to have full orbits, with eight in the outer one. In chemical reactions, atoms lose, gain or share electrons in order to end up with full orbits. Atoms with full orbits are very stable, because they don't need to react with other atoms. They already have the right number of electrons.

What happens in a chemical reaction?

Sodium chloride, or table salt, is a very stable compound. It is made up of sodium, an alkali metal, and chlorine, a halogen, both of which are extremely reactive groups of elements. If you look at the structure of their atoms, you can see why.

Sodium has two full orbits, but its outer orbit has only one electron – which it will happily get rid of.

Chlorine has seven electrons in its outer orbit. So it needs one more to make it stable.

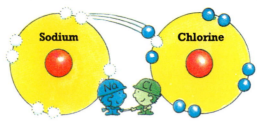

When they react together, chlorine takes the extra electron from sodium. It fills its own orbit and leaves sodium with full orbits too. This way both atoms are satisfied.

Atom puzzle

Which metal atoms do you think might react with which non-metal atoms?

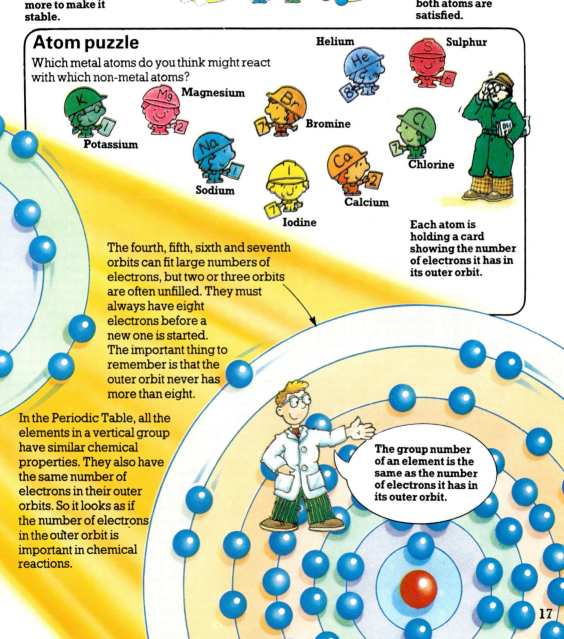

Each atom is holding a card showing the number of electrons it has in its outer orbit.

The fourth, fifth, sixth and seventh orbits can fit large numbers of electrons, but two or three orbits are often unfilled. They must always have eight electrons before a new one is started. The important thing to remember is that the outer orbit never has more than eight.

In the Periodic Table, all the elements in a vertical group have similar chemical properties. They also have the same number of electrons in their outer orbits. So it looks as if the number of electrons in the outer orbit is important in chemical reactions.

The group number of an element is the same as the number of electrons it has in its outer orbit.

Looking at compounds

To understand more about how compounds are formed, you could try testing a few different ones. Here are some experiments you could do with butter, wax, lard, sodium chloride (salt), sodium carbonate (washing powder) and sodium hydrogen carbonate (bicarbonate of soda). Make a chart and write down your results.

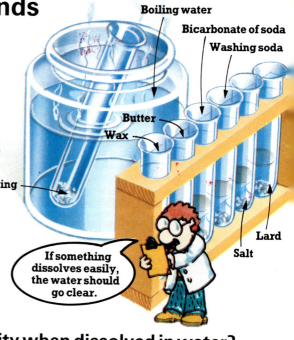

Which ones melt easily?
Put a test tube containing each compound into a beaker of boiling water.

Which ones dissolve easily?
Put a little of each compound into separate test tubes of cold water and stir it. Use enough to cover the end of a spoon handle.

Which ones conduct electricity when dissolved in water?
If something conducts electricity, it means it allows electricity to pass through it. Put a little of each compound into separate jars of distilled water.* Set up your apparatus like this. Dip the electrodes into each one. If the bulb lights up, it means that electricity is being conducted.

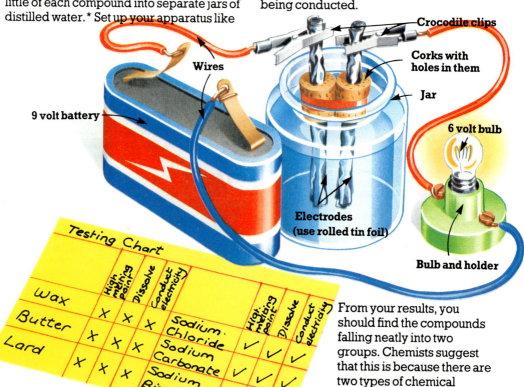

From your results, you should find the compounds falling neatly into two groups. Chemists suggest that this is because there are two types of chemical bonding. You will find out more about this on the next few pages.

*You can buy this at the chemist, or at a garage.

Looking at your results

One of the groups of compounds all contained sodium. As you know, sodium is highly reactive, because it has one electron that it wants to lose. When it reacts with another element, it loses this electron. This makes it positively charged, because it then has more protons than electrons. An atom that has lost electrons is called a positive ion. Atoms which gain electrons in a reaction are called negative ions. When positive and negative ions join together, an ionic or electrovalent bond is formed. The ions attract each other because of their opposite charges. This makes the bond very strong, and so ionic compounds are difficult to melt. They are usually solids.

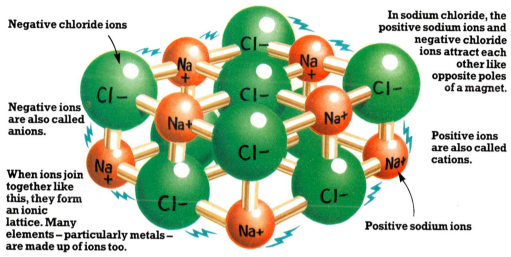

Negative chloride ions

Negative ions are also called anions.

When ions join together like this, they form an ionic lattice. Many elements – particularly metals – are made up of ions too.

In sodium chloride, the positive sodium ions and negative chloride ions attract each other like opposite poles of a magnet.

Positive ions are also called cations.

Positive sodium ions

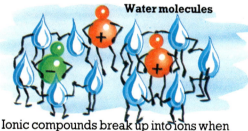

Water molecules

Ionic compounds break up into ions when they are in water. This is why they dissolve easily. Water molecules are strongly attracted to ions and can push their way between them.

Spotting ionic compounds

Ionic compounds are usually made up of a metal and a non-metal. They are made by combining an element which loses electrons easily (on the left of the Periodic Table) with an element which gains electrons easily (on the right of the Periodic Table).

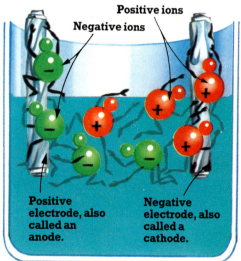

Positive ions
Negative ions

Positive electrode, also called an anode.
Negative electrode, also called a cathode.

Ionic compounds are good conductors of electricity because they contain charged particles, or ions. Electricity is the flow of charged particles. When the electricity is switched on, the negative ions all tend to flow towards the positive electrode, and the positive ions towards the negative electrode.

Covalent compounds

The other group of compounds in your experiment all contain carbon and hydrogen. If you look at the structure of carbon, you will see that it has four electrons in its outer orbit. This makes it hard to decide whether to lose or gain electrons, in order to fill its orbits. So it doesn't do either. Instead it shares electrons with the atoms of the other elements. When elements share electrons, a covalent compound is formed. Covalent compounds do not conduct heat or electricity, because they do not contain charged particles (ions).

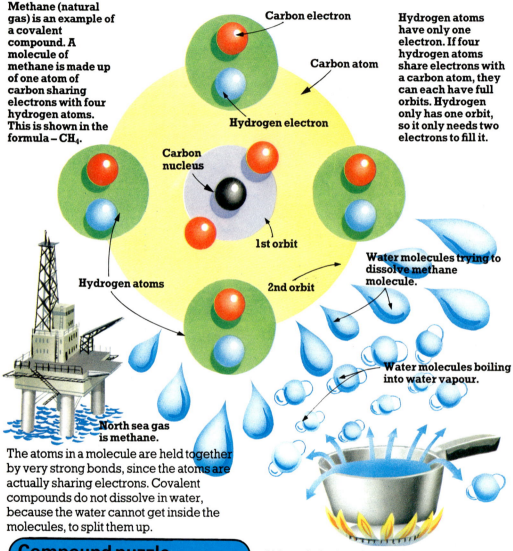

Methane (natural gas) is an example of a covalent compound. A molecule of methane is made up of one atom of carbon sharing electrons with four hydrogen atoms. This is shown in the formula – CH_4.

Carbon electron

Carbon atom

Hydrogen electron

Carbon nucleus

1st orbit

2nd orbit

Hydrogen atoms

Hydrogen atoms have only one electron. If four hydrogen atoms share electrons with a carbon atom, they can each have full orbits. Hydrogen only has one orbit, so it only needs two electrons to fill it.

Water molecules trying to dissolve methane molecule.

Water molecules boiling into water vapour.

North sea gas is methane.

The atoms in a molecule are held together by very strong bonds, since the atoms are actually sharing electrons. Covalent compounds do not dissolve in water, because the water cannot get inside the molecules, to split them up.

Compound puzzle
Now that you know about the properties of the two different types of compounds, see if you can work out which group these ones belong to. You could try the same tests as before.

Sugar   **Methylated spirits**

Bicycle oil   **Epsom salts**

Although the bonds within a molecule are strong, the bonds between molecules are relatively weak. This makes them easier to separate than ions, which are held tightly in lattices. Covalent compounds have low boiling or melting points, because they don't need as much energy (in the form of heat) to push the molecules apart. They are mostly liquids, such as water, or gases.

Valencies

The number of electrons that an atom needs to gain, lose or share in a chemical reaction is called its valency. The valency of an element is sometimes called its "combining power". Some elements have more than one valency, because they combine in different ways. There is a list of valencies of common elements on page 45. You can guess the valency of an element by looking at its atomic structure.

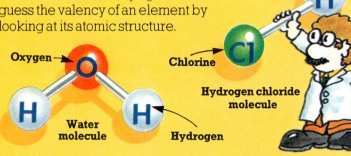

Each bar represents a pair of electrons being shared. (These are all covalent compounds.)

Hydrogen has only one electron, and only one to gain, so it must have a valency of one. You can work out the valencies of other elements from the way they combine with hydrogen. For example, in a water molecule, the oxygen atom shares two electrons with the hydrogen atoms. So the valency of oxygen is two.* Using these compounds, see if you can work out the valencies of carbon, nitrogen and chlorine. The valency is the same as the number of bars coming out of each atom.

Working out formulae from valencies

The proportion of different elements in a compound is shown in its formula. This proportion depends on the valencies of the elements. To form a compound, the total valencies of each element must add up to the same number. If, like chlorine and hydrogen, the elements have the same valency, then they combine in equal proportions. The formula is a simple one, with no numbers in it. If the elements have different valencies, you have to multiply one or both of them, so that they are equal. You can work out the formula of a compound if you know the valencies of its elements.

Carbon: valency 4
Oxygen: valency 2

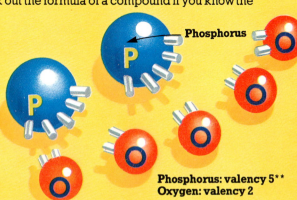

Phosphorus: valency 5**
Oxygen: valency 2

For example, look at carbon and oxygen. You can make their valencies equal if you multiply oxygen by two. You show this is the formula by writing a small $_2$ after the O. So carbon and oxygen form the compound, carbon dioxide – CO_2.

Combining phosphorus and oxygen is more complicated. You have to multiply phosphorus by two and oxygen by five, so that they both add up to ten. They combine to form phosphorus pentoxide, which has the formula P_2O_5.

*You can check this by looking at its atomic structure.
**Phosphorus sometimes has a valency of three.

Fast and slow reactions

Some chemical reactions take seconds, others take hundreds, or thousands, of years. Caves and potholes are made by a slow chemical reaction. Rain reacts with carbon dioxide in the air, to produce small amounts of weak carbonic acid in the raindrops. When rain falls, it reacts with limestone rocks, wearing them away slowly. Over centuries, it cuts deep grooves in the rock, which eventually form caves.

Fumes from traffic and factory chimneys give off chemicals into the air, which also react with the rain. This produces nitric and sulphuric acid in the rain. These are stronger and much more harmful than carbonic acid. "Acid rain" is killing off forests in some parts of the world.

The acropolis in Athens has been standing for over two thousand years. It is made of marble (another form of calcium carbonate), which has been slowly worn away over the years by wind and rain. This reaction has been speeded up recently by chemical pollution in the atmosphere.

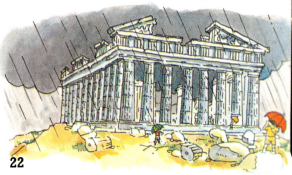

Speeding up a reaction

Here is an experiment which shows how you can speed up or slow down a reaction. You need to do the same experiment several times, using exactly the same quantities of ingredients each time. Set up your equipment as shown in the picture. The small test tube contains hydrochloric acid. The larger one contains some marble chips.
To start the reaction, you shake the larger tube, so that the ingredients mix. The measuring tube should be full of water when you start. Turn it upside down and put it in a bowl of water, holding something over it as you do so, to stop the water falling out.

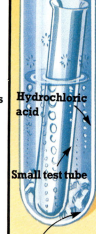

Cork

Large test tube

Hydrochloric acid

Small test tube

Marble chips

1

Spirit burner

Methylated spirits

Then try the same experiment using acid that has been warmed first. This should make the reaction quicker. The same thing happens to food. It goes bad quite quickly in hot weather. In a freezer you can stop it going bad for months.

2

22

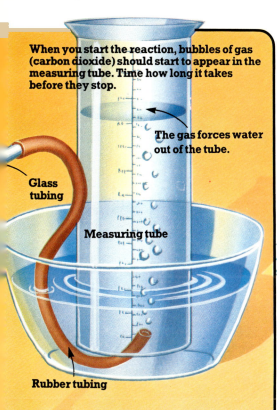

When you start the reaction, bubbles of gas (carbon dioxide) should start to appear in the measuring tube. Time how long it takes before they stop.

The gas forces water out of the tube.

Glass tubing

Measuring tube

Rubber tubing

In your last experiment, try using smaller pieces of marble. Grind them into a fine powder with a rolling pin.

3

Lumps of coal do not react with air unless they are heated. However, coal dust and air can react together, causing explosions in coal mines.

Slowing down a reaction

In the next experiment, try diluting the acid with water. This should make the reaction slower. The acid which helps to erode the caves is diluted with a lot of rain. This is why they take so long to form.

What makes reactions faster?

When you heat something, you give the particles more energy, so they can move faster. The faster they move, the quicker the reaction. In a car crash, the faster the cars are going, the sooner they will collide. Tortoises travelling towards each other would take much longer to meet. And if they bumped into each other, they would hardly bruise themselves at all.

Smaller pieces of a substance react faster because they allow more of that substance to come into immediate contact with the other substance. In the picture below, the blue blobs take longer to get inside the large red blob than to get inside the smaller red blobs. So the reaction is slower.

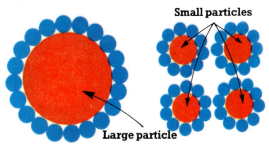

Small particles

Large particle

The substances which take part in a reaction are called reactants. The more concentrated the reactants are, the faster the reaction will be, because there are more particles available for the reaction. When a substance is diluted, it takes longer for the particles to find each other.

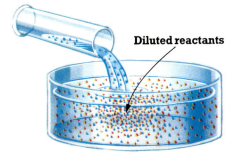

Diluted reactants

23

Catalysts

A catalyst is something which alters the speed of a reaction, without being permanently changed itself. Some reactions would take years, without the presence of a catalyst.

Here is an experiment you can do using a catalyst. It shows hydrogen peroxide splitting up into oxygen and water. You don't need heat to start this reaction. Hydrogen peroxide reacts when it is exposed to light.

Set up your equipment as shown in the picture. At the start of the experiment, the test tube should be full of water. Fill it up and keep your thumb over the top as you turn it upside down. There should be enough water in the bowl underneath to cover the opening of the test tube.

As a catalyst, you could use a small piece of liver, or some manganese IV oxide.* Weigh the catalyst before you start. Then dry it and weigh it again after the experiment – to show that it has not been affected.

Add the catalyst to the hydrogen peroxide. Within minutes, small bubbles of oxygen should start to collect in the tube. They force water out of the top of the tube and into the bowl below.

The water level in the bowl will rise. If you let the reaction go on for a long time, the tube will empty and the bowl may overflow.

Use something to prop up the test tube, so that it doesn't fall over.

Here is a test to make sure that the gas is oxygen. Light a splint of wood. Then blow it out, making sure that it is still glowing. Press your thumb over the test tube and remove it from the bowl. Then put the glowing splint into the tube. If the gas is oxygen, rather than just ordinary air, it should burst into flame.

To show that the catalyst has worked, set up the experiment as before, but without the catalyst. Use the same amount of hydrogen peroxide. How long is it before you get a reaction?

Catalysts are used a lot in industry, in the production of such things as petrol, margarine and ammonia. Catalysts are usually made from heavy or transition metals and come in the form of pellets, like these.

*This is one of several compounds made from manganese and oxygen.

How catalysts work

The energy needed to start a reaction is called "activation energy". A catalyst works by lowering the amount of activation energy needed. So the reaction starts sooner. Imagine the activation energy as a sort of hump on a hillside. You have to ride over the hump in order to get down the other side – but if you find another path, which avoids the hump, you will be able to get there sooner.

Enzymes

Enzymes are extremely complex chemicals, some of which live in the cells in your body. Amongst other things, they help you digest your food. Enzymes are a sort of catalyst. They often work by breaking bigger molecules into smaller ones. Enzymes are used as catalysts in making cheese, beer, wine, and other things. Biological washing powders contain enzymes which can "eat up" protein stains such as blood. Enzymes are less versatile than other catalysts, so they can only work at certain temperatures.

Watch an enzyme at work

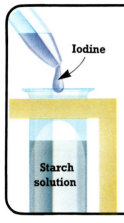

If you add iodine to starch, it will go blue. Take two test tubes and put a piece of starch in each (potato or bread). Put some saliva in one of them. Leave them in a warm place for a few days, then test both the tubes with iodine. One goes blue, the other doesn't. What has happened? The answer is that saliva contains an enzyme, called amylase, which breaks down starch into glucose. If you add iodine to glucose, it doesn't go blue.

How metals react

Some metals are highly reactive; others hardly react at all. The very reactive ones are hardly ever found on their own. They form very stable compounds, which are difficult to split. You can find out how reactive a metal is by looking at the activity series, shown below. It lists metals according to how reactive they are with air and water.*

Potassium and sodium are so reactive, they have to be stored in oil – away from contact with the air. In water, potassium catches alight and burns with a pinkish purple flame.

Aluminium reacts with air to form a thin, almost invisible coat, which protects it from water. This is why planes are made of aluminium.

Zinc reacts very slowly with water. Metals, such as iron, are often coated with zinc – or "galvanized" – to stop rust.

Iron rusts.

Copper, silver and gold are very unreactive. This is why they are used for jewellery. Tutankhamun's gold mask has survived thousands of years.

Oxidation

The activity series can help you understand why some reactions happen.

When an element reacts with oxygen, it produces a compound called an oxide. Chemists call this oxidation. Rust is partly a form of oxidation. Metals lower on the list, such as copper, do not react easily with oxygen. They have to be heated with air to make them react. When a substance burns in oxygen, the reaction is called combustion.

Eating and breathing are also a form of combustion. The food you eat is burnt up inside your body by the oxygen you breathe. This produces energy which you can use.

What makes things rust?

Rust is a common chemical reaction, which happens to iron and metals containing iron. Try this experiment to find out what causes it. You need five test tubes with a little wire wool in each. Then add the following:

1. Tap water.

2. Boiled water. (Boiling removes the air bubbles from water. Press the cork right down to stop more air getting in.)

3. Test tube left open, so that air can get in. (Air contains water vapour.)

4. Tap water and salt.

5. Dry air. You can remove water vapour from air by putting a little calcium chloride in the tube, and sealing it.

You will need to leave the tubes for at least a day before you see a reaction. Tube number four should rust first. Rust is caused by a combination of water and air, speeded up by salt. Tubes two and five will only rust if air and water vapour get through the cork into the tube.

*The activity series is listed on page 47.

What is burning?

When a substance gives out energy in the form of heat and light, we say that it is burning. Burning is a form of oxidation, because it requires oxygen. Without oxygen, nothing would burn. Most things need to be given energy, by being heated to a certain temperature, before they can burn.

Why can nothing burn on the Moon?
(See page 45.)

Reduction

Reduction is the opposite of oxidation. When something gives oxygen to another substance, chemists say it has been reduced. The other substance has been oxidized. So oxidation and reduction usually happen in the same reaction. Metals high in the series react strongly with oxygen and can remove oxygen from metals lower down the list. This doesn't only apply to removing oxygen. If you add a metal to a solution of a compound containing a less reactive metal, it will "push" the less reactive metal out of the solution.

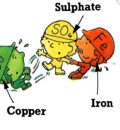

Try leaving an iron nail in a solution of copper sulphate. The copper will collect around the nail, turning it pink. This is because the iron has "pushed" the copper out of the solution. Chemists call this a displacement reaction.

Flame tests

When some metals burn, they produce a distinctive coloured flame. This can help you work out whether a particular metal is present in an unknown compound. You need an unreactive wire, such as nichrome, which will not interfere in the experiment. Dip it in hydrochloric acid to clean it, then heat it red hot. When no colour is added to the flame, dip it in the unknown compound and heat it again.

Calcium
Copper
Sodium
Lithium
Potassium
Barium

Fireworks are made from compounds containing calcium, strontium (crimson) and barium.

Acids, bases and salts

Acids, bases and salts are three very important groups of chemicals. You can fit most compounds into one or other of these groups. Acids are compounds which produce hydrogen ions when in water. (Remember, ions are atoms which have lost or gained electrons.) Most acids contain oxygen too, as part of an acid radical* ion. Bases are usually metal oxides and hydroxides. Salts are made up of metal ions and acid radical ions. Most compounds ending in -ide, -ite or -ate are salts (except oxides and hydroxides).

All the things on the right contain acids, though some are stronger than others. All acids have a sour taste and strong smell. But never taste chemicals. Strong acids burn and sting, and can even dissolve metals.

Vinegar, Car batteries, Lemons, Tea leaves, Ants, Nettles

Washing soda, Wasps, Oven cleaner, Caustic soda, Potash, Indigestion tablets

Bases are chemically opposite to acids. Bases that are soluble in water are called alkalis. They have a bitter taste and feel soapy. Strong alkalis burn your skin and can dissolve things. The things on the left all contain alkalis.

Testing acids and alkalis

You can decide whether something is an acid or alkali by using an indicator, such as litmus paper. Acids turn blue litmus red. Alkalis turn red litmus blue.

ACID — ALKALI

Chemists use a range of numbers, called pH numbers, to describe how acid or alkaline something is. Acids range from 1 to 6; alkalis from 8 to 14. 7 is neutral. With "universal indicator" papers, the colours change gradually according to the strength of the acid or alkali. (The actual shades vary a little according to the make of indicator.)

1 2 3 4 5 6 7 8 9 10 11 12 13 14

STRONGLY ACIDIC | WEAKLY ACIDIC | NEUTRAL | WEAKLY ALKALINE | STRONGLY ALKALINE

If you can get some universal indicator, you could try to find the pH numbers of a few different compounds: apple juice, paraffin, toothpaste, salt, sugar, ammonia. (Dissolve any solids in water first.)

*A radical is a group of elements, which behaves as a single element, such as CO_3 – carbonate.

Neutralization

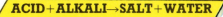
ACID + ALKALI → SALT + WATER

If you mix together the right quantities of acid and alkali, they neutralize one another and produce a neutral salt. Neutral salts do not burn, like acids and alkalis. The salt you eat is one type of salt, but there are many others.

You could try making some salt yourself. Pour a little dilute hydrochloric  acid into a jar. Test it with blue litmus paper – which should turn red. Then add dilute sodium hydroxide, a drop at a time. When the litmus turns blue again, add a bit more acid, until the paper turns purple. Then boil away some of the liquid, leaving the rest to evaporate. Then you should be left with salt crystals.

Other neutralization reactions

If you put lemon juice on your tongue, it will taste sour. Then try adding a pinch of baking powder. It neutralizes the acid, so that it doesn't taste sour any longer.

Indigestion happens because too much acid is released into your stomach when you over eat. Indigestion tablets contain a mild alkali to cure this.

You can soothe acid bee stings with bicarbonate of soda, an alkali.

Some plants like an alkaline soil, others, an acid one. Hydrangeas will only produce pink or white flowers in an alkaline soil. If you add a special compound to make the soil more acidic, you will produce blue flowers.

More reactions with acids

ACID + METAL → SALT + HYDROGEN

Acids react with metals to give off hydrogen, providing the metal is higher in the activity series than hydrogen. The metal is replacing the hydrogen in the acid, because it is more reactive. Pour some hydrochloric acid on to some granulated zinc.* Bubbles of gas should appear. Keep your finger over the tube to trap the gas. Then test for hydrogen by inserting a lighted splint. If it is hydrogen, it should burn with a "pop".

ACID + CARBONATE → SALT + CARBON DIOXIDE

Acids react with carbonates to give off carbon dioxide. You may have seen this happening if you did the experiment on page 22. A similar sort of reaction happens inside a cake. Baking powder contains tartaric acid and sodium hydrogen carbonate. When they are heated they react together to produce bubbles of carbon dioxide inside the cake.

*Always add the acid to the other chemical, not the other way around.

What is organic chemistry?

Organic chemistry is the study of compounds containing carbon.* It is called "organic", because chemists used to think that these compounds could only be found in living organisms. All living things do contain carbon, but so do plastics, medicines, artifical fabrics and many other man-made substances. So it is really just a convenient way of dividing up chemistry.

Carbon compounds are often made up of very large, sometimes giant, molecules, containing hundreds, or even thousands, of atoms. This is because carbon atoms form very stable, covalent bonds with other atoms, and can link themselves into long chains and rings. Organic compounds usually contain only a few other elements – such as hydrogen and oxygen. But there are so many different possible combinations, that they can form a great variety of different compounds.

Testing organic compounds

All foods are organic compounds. When they are burnt they often go black – like coal, which is a form of carbon. They give off carbon dioxide.

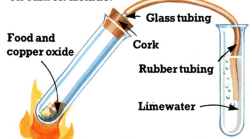

Carbon dioxide turns limewater milky. So test this by bubbling it through limewater. To make the limewater, dissolve some calcium hydroxide in water. Some of it will settle on the bottom. Then pour the top, clear liquid into a test tube.

The same thing happens when you eat. There is a lot of organic chemistry going on inside you. Your body burns the food and you breathe out carbon dioxide. Blow through a straw into the limewater.** What happens?

Digestion

Food is mostly made up of huge molecules of carbohydrates, proteins and fats. These are broken down into much smaller molecules by digestion. Digestion is carried out by organic catalysts, called enzymes, in the mouth, stomach and digestive tract. Here are examples of a few of the different enzymes.

This is a starch molecule. A lot of foods contain starch – bread, potatoes, cakes, vegetables. It is made up of smaller molecules of glucose, linked together.

Starch molecule

Amylase attacks starches

Amylase

*A few simple compounds, such as carbon dioxide, are not counted as organic.
**Make sure you don't breathe in!

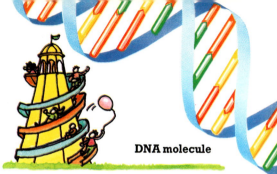
DNA molecule

DNA

One very interesting organic compound is DNA (deoxyribonucleic acid), a substance which is found in all living cells. In 1954, in Cambridge, two scientists, Francis Crick and James Watson, worked out the structure of its molecules. Each one is shaped in a double helix – rather like two helter skelters wound round each other.

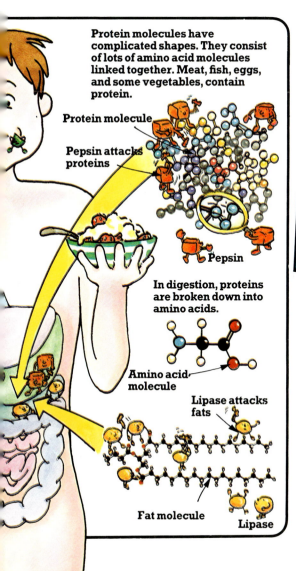

Protein molecules have complicated shapes. They consist of lots of amino acid molecules linked together. Meat, fish, eggs, and some vegetables, contain protein.

Protein molecule

Pepsin attacks proteins

Pepsin

In digestion, proteins are broken down into amino acids.

Amino acid molecule

Lipase attacks fats

Fat molecule

Lipase

Fermentation

Fermentation is a way of breaking down carbohydrates, by means of enzymes and a fungus called yeast. Fermentation produces alcohol. There are many different types of alcohol. The one found in alcoholic drinks is called ethanol.

Making wine

You could try fermenting some fruit juice. Mix together a carton of fruit juice, about 200g of sugar, a pinch of yeast and some water.

Put it in a corked container. Insert a glass tube in the top, with the end in a jar of limewater. This allows carbon dioxide to escape, without letting oxygen in.

Leave in a warm place for a few days. You should see the limewater going milky, showing that carbon dioxide has been given off. You will need to leave it for a few weeks before it ferments properly.

Alcohols react with oxygen to produce organic acids. If you leave a bottle of wine open for a few days, it will become oxidized by the air. The result is ethanoic acid, which tastes sour. This is the acid you get in vinegar.

Organic families

Organic compounds can be divided into well-defined groups and families. The simplest of these groups is the hydrocarbons. The hydrocarbons are divided into families, such as the alkanes, with similar chemical properties. Their properties change gradually according to the size of the molecule.

Alkanes

Here are the first six members of the alkane family. It starts with methane, which is the simplest organic compound. Like all hydrocarbons, each alkane increases in size according to a set pattern.* Alkanes are fairly unreactive. Chemists call them saturated compounds, because they have enough hydrogen atoms to go round. They all have single bonds. The first part of the name of a hydrocarbon tells you how many atoms it has.**

Alkanes with less than four carbons are gases. Between five and 16, they are liquids, such as petrol. With more than 16 carbons, they are solids, such as candle wax.

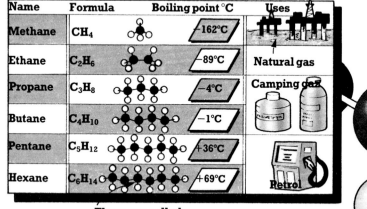

Name	Formula		Boiling point °C	Uses
Methane	CH_4		−162°C	
Ethane	C_2H_6		−89°C	Natural gas
Propane	C_3H_8		−4°C	Camping gaz
Butane	C_4H_{10}		−1°C	
Pentane	C_5H_{12}		+36°C	
Hexane	C_6H_{14}		+69°C	Petrol

These are called unbranched chains.

Isomers

Isomers are compounds which have the same formula as each other, but different structures. So they still have the same number of atoms of each element, but they are arranged in different ways. This is methylpropane, an isomer of butane. Unlike butane, it has a branched chain structure. Count up the atoms, and you will see that they have exactly the same number. But their structures make them behave differently.

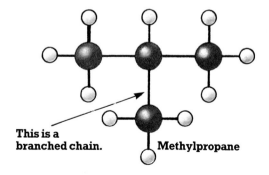

This is a branched chain.

Methylpropane

Make a molecular model

Chemists often build molecular models, to help them see what might happen in a chemical reaction. This is very important when you are dealing with complicated molecules. They are very difficult to draw two-dimensionally on paper. You could try to make a model of ethanol. You need matches and some plasticine. Make two large black balls, six small white ones and a red one.

Take one of the black balls (carbon) and stick four matches into it – in the shape of a tetrahedron.

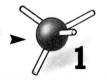

Repeat this with the other one, then remove one of the sticks. Join the two carbon atoms together, using the hole you have just made.

Attach white balls (hydrogens) to the ends of five of the sticks, and a red one (oxygen) to the sixth one.

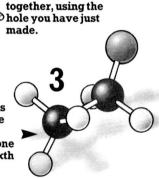

*This is expressed in the formula C_nH_{2n+2}.
**From the fifth onwards, the names are based on the Latin word for each number.

Alkenes

The alkenes are another family of hydrocarbons. They have two fewer hydrogen atoms in each molecule than each equivalent alkane. Alkenes are said to be unsaturated, because they contain double bonds. This means that the carbon atoms share two pairs of electrons with each other. Alkenes are fairly reactive, because of this "spare" bond which could be joined to another atom.

Double bond

This is ethene, the simplest alkene.

Polymers

Polymers are giant molecules, made by linking lots of smaller, identical molecules together. These smaller molecules are called monomers. They contain double or triple bonds, which are removed when the molecules become linked to each other. This is called polymerization. A lot of polymers come from natural substances, such as cellulose, which is found in plants.

Polyethene molecules contain up to 50,000 atoms.

Carbon

Hydrogen

This is polyethene, another name for the plastic, polythene. It is made by adding lots of ethene molecules together.

Polymer comes from the Greek, meaning "many parts".

Alkynes

Alkynes are even more reactive than alkenes. They have four fewer hydrogen atoms than they need in each molecule. So the carbon atoms have to share three pairs of electrons. This is called a triple bond.

Triple bond

To complete the model, put another stick in the oxygen atom, and put a hydrogen on the end.

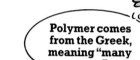

4

See if you can make an isomer of ethanol. Take your model apart and join up all the atoms in a different way, using all the same holes. Find the answer on page 47.

Cyclic hydrocarbons

A few hydrocarbons, such as benzene, contain atoms held in rings. This structure was discovered by a 19th-century German chemist, called Kekulé. Some people at the time made fun of the idea by drawing a ring made up of six monkeys. They joined hands to form single bonds, and tails to form double bonds.

Benzene

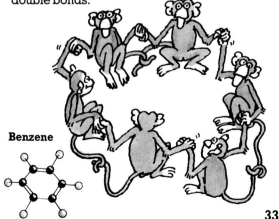

33

Useful organic compounds

Crude oil

Crude oil contains lots of alkanes, which have different boiling points. It can be separated into many useful chemical products in a process called fractional distillation. The oil is heated and the products, known as fractions, are collected at different temperatures.

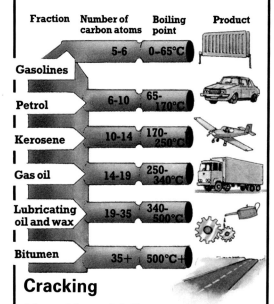

Fraction	Number of carbon atoms	Boiling point	Product
Gasolines	5-6	0-65°C	
Petrol	6-10	65-170°C	
Kerosene	10-14	170-250°C	
Gas oil	14-19	250-340°C	
Lubricating oil and wax	19-35	340-500°C	
Bitumen	35+	500°C+	

Cracking

Many of the useful alkanes, such as petrol, are made up of small molecules with low boiling points. Crude oil contains a lot of alkanes with larger molecules and high boiling points. There isn't enough of the fraction containing petrol to satisfy world demand. However, chemists have found a way of breaking these heavier alkanes into shorter, lighter ones. It is done by heating them to very high temperatures with a catalyst. This process is called cracking.

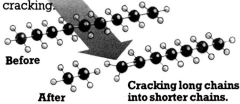

Before

After

Cracking long chains into shorter chains.

One of the best ingredients of petrol is 2,2,4-Trimethyl pentane (once called iso-octane). The "octane" rating is used as a way of grading petrol. The higher the octane, the better the petrol.

Plastics

Plastics are a group of polymers which are mostly man-made. They have qualities that are extremely useful. They are strong, easy to colour and clean. They keep in warmth and insulate against electricity. They do not usually rot or wear away.

There are two main types of plastics – thermoplastics and themosets. Thermoplastics include polyethene, PVC, nylon and polystyrene. They are made up of molecules in straight, unlinked chains. They can be heated, moulded and hardened over and over again.

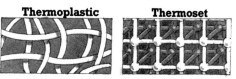

Thermoplastic   Thermoset

Thermosets are brittle and do not melt. Their molecules are linked in chains and set hard. They cannot be remoulded. Formica and bakelite (the first plastic, invented in 1933), are thermosets.

Make your own plastic

Warm some day-old milk in a pan (skim the top of the milk off first). Add some vinegar, a drop at a time. A white elastic substance is formed.

Identifying plastics

TEST for...	PVC	POLY STYRENE	POLY THENE
Does it break/cut easily?	With scissors	Breaks when hit with a hammer	With scissors
Does it bend easily?	No	Does not bend	Some bend easily, others dont
Does it float?	No	Yes	Yes
Is it softened by heat?	Yes	Yes	Yes
How does it burn?	With difficulty. Produces white, acrid fumes and a yellow flame. Does not burn long.	Easily. Produces sooty smoke with a flowery smell and a deep yellow flame. Continues to burn.	Easily. Produces yellow/blue flame and little smoke. Smells waxy and continues to burn.

BEWARE FUMES!

Fats and margarines

Animal fats and vegetable oils belong to a group of compounds called esters. Esters are made by mixing an organic acid with an alcohol. Fats can be solid or liquid. They are insoluble in water, but soluble in many organic solvents, such as dry-cleaning fluid. They float, as they are less dense than water.

What are polyunsaturates?

Some margarines are advertised as having polyunsaturated fats. This means the molecules contain many (poly) double or triple bonds, because they do not have enough hydrogen. Polyunsaturated fats are supposed to be healthier and reduce the risk of heart disease. They are almost liquid at room temperature and spread like butter. Adding hydrogen, to reduce the double bonds, makes them solid but saturated.

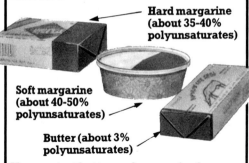

Hard margarine (about 35-40% polyunsaturates)

Soft margarine (about 40-50% polyunsaturates)

Butter (about 3% polyunsaturates)

You can test butter and margarine by using iodine and an organic solvent.

Add some iodine to each test tube, drop by drop. The unsaturated molecules will react with iodine and absorb the colour. When the colour reappears, it means that the solution is saturated. Count how many drops it takes for this to happen.

What is soap?

Soap is really a kind of salt. It is a sodium or potassium salt, made by combining an organic acid with an alkali.

How soap works

Water often seems to have a sort of skin which allows things to float on it. This is called surface tension. It happens because water molecules are very strongly attracted to one another. Water and oil do not mix, so water isn't attracted to molecules of greasy dirt. Soaps and detergents work by lowering the surface tension, so that the water will spread more easily over the things you want to wash.

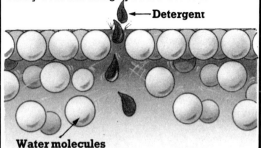

Soap molecules are made up of two parts – a long hydrocarbon tail, which repels water, and a head made up of charged ions, which attracts water. By attracting water, the ions reduce the attraction water molecules have for each other.

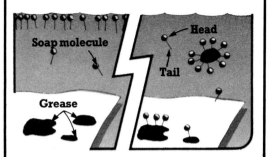

The hydrocarbon tail is attracted to the dirt and grease in the clothes. The tail sticks into the dirt, and at the same time, the water-loving head pulls away from the clothes towards the water. This pulls the grease out of the clothes.

Splitting compounds

Before the reaction

Although the elements in a compound are bonded chemically, most compounds can be split by some means or another. A reaction in which a compound is split is called a decomposition reaction. You will already have come across examples of these earlier in this section. All replacement reactions, such as the one with copper sulphate and iron*, involve the splitting of a compound.

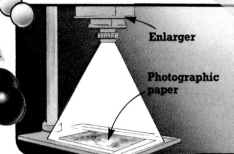

To split a compound, you nearly always need some kind of energy. A few compounds will split up after being exposed to light. Silver chloride, for example, is used in the production of photographic paper and film, because of its sensitivity to light. Some compounds will split up after being heated. Mercury oxide, for example, decomposes to form mercury and oxygen when you heat it.

After the reaction

Double decomposition

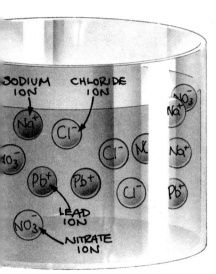
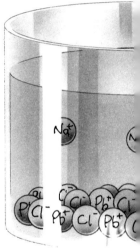

Double decomposition is when two compounds split up and swap partners. Most salts are soluble in water, but some are not. When you dissolve salts in water, they split up into separate ions. If two salts swap their partner ions, an insoluble salt may be produced. The insoluble salt forms a "precipitate", a solid which settles at the bottom. This is also called a precipitation reaction. Sodium chloride and lead nitrate are both soluble salts. When you dissolve them together, they swap partners and lead chloride forms a precipitate.

Solubility Guide

* All nitrates are soluble.
* All potassium, sodium and ammonium salts are soluble in water.
* All carbonates are insoluble, except sodium, potassium and ammonium.
* All sulphates are soluble in water except barium, lead, silver and calcium.
* All chlorides are soluble, except silver and lead.
* All bromides are soluble, except silver and lead.

If sodium carbonate and zinc sulphate are dissolved in water and swap partners, which one will be the precipitate? Use this chart. It shows which salts are soluble and which are not.

*You can find this reaction on page 27.

Electrolysis

The most reactive elements require a great deal of energy to release them from their compounds. One method is to pass electricity through them. This is called electrolysis. Substances that allow electricity to pass through them are called electrolytes. All ionic compounds are electrolytes, when molten*, or in solution.

How electrolysis works

When the electricity is switched on, electrons flow through the wires, bulb and battery. They travel from the positive electrode towards the negative electrode. The compound splits into positive and negative ions. The negative ions travel towards the positive electrode, and the positive ions towards the negative electrode. This is because they are attracted by opposite charges. At the electrodes, the positive ions receive electrons and the negative ions lose electrons. This way, they are both turned back into "neutral" atoms.

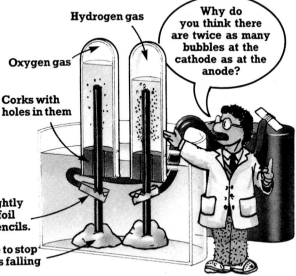

Why do you think there are twice as many bubbles at the cathode as at the anode?

Hydrogen gas
Oxygen gas
Corks with holes in them
Electrodes. Use tightly rolled aluminium foil or the insides of pencils.
Plasticine to stop electrodes falling over

Splitting water

Water contains positive hydrogen ions and negative oxygen ions. You can split water by using electrolysis. When you put the electrodes in the water, bubbles will start to appear around them. You can test these gases by putting a glowing piece of wood at the bottom of the tube. Remember, oxygen will relight it; hydrogen makes it go "pop".

Using electrolysis

Electrolysis has many uses in industry. It is used for extracting highly reactive metals from their compounds. It is also used for plating things with another metal. This is how silver-plated cutlery is made. The knife or fork is put at the cathode, while a silver compound is electrolysed. The silver ions flow towards the cathode, coating the knife with silver.

Electrolysis and the activity series

If a mixture of compounds is electrolysed, the ions of the least reactive elements will be turned back into atoms first. This is because they don't need as much energy to split them from their compounds. If you electrolyse a compound in water, the metal will only be deposited at the cathode if it is lower than hydrogen** in the activity series. If not, hydrogen ions from the water will be deposited there instead. All highly reactive metals, such as sodium, have to be electrolysed in a molten state.

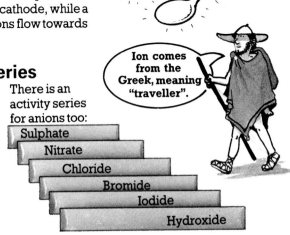

There is an activity series for anions too:
Sulphate
Nitrate
Chloride
Bromide
Iodide
Hydroxide

Ion comes from the Greek, meaning "traveller".

The ones at the bottom of the list will be deposited at the anode first.

*Molten means melted.   **Hydrogen is not a metal, but it is included in the activity series.

Identifying substances

Here are some clues to help you guess the identity of an unknown substance. You could try out these tests on a chemical from a chemistry set. There isn't room to include all the tests that chemists do, but these ones will help you identify quite a few common chemicals. You can find the instructions for most of these tests explained earlier in the book. If you can't remember how to do them, you could look them up in the index.

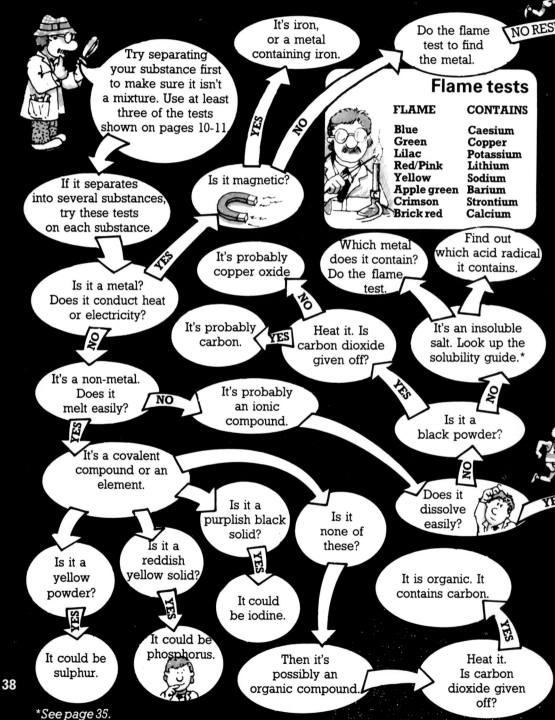

*See page 35.

Borax bead test

Heat a loop of platinum wire ** and then dip it in distilled water. Dip it in sodium borate and heat the wire until you get a glass-like "bead". Add a bit of the unknown substance and heat it again. Substances containing certain metals produce different coloured beads. The colours depend on whether you have heated it on the inside or outside part of the flame.

No result? Try the Borax bead test.

INSIDE FLAME	OUTSIDE FLAME	Contains
Blue		Chromium
Green		Cobalt
Red/Brown	Turquoise	Copper
Dark green	Yellow	Iron
Pale green	Purple	Manganese
Black	Red/Brown	Nickel

Is it acidic, alkaline or neutral? Use an indicator to find out.

ACIDIC → It's acidic. Is it an acid or an acidic salt. Heat it with zinc. Does it give off hydrogen?

- **YES →** It's an acid! Which one? Do the ACID RADICAL TESTS.
  - Does it give a white precipitate when added to barium chloride? **YES →** The acid radical is sulphate. → It's sulphuric acid.
  - Does it give a white precipitate when added to silver nitrate? **YES →** The acid radical is chloride. → It's hydrochloric acid.
  - Does it give off carbon dioxide when heated. → The acid radical is carbonate. → It's carbonic acid or a carbonate.
  - Find out which metal it contains. Do the flame tests.
  - Combine the metal and the acid radical to get the name of the compound.*

- **NO →** It's an acidic salt.
  - Which acid radical does it contain? Do the acid radical tests.
  - Do the flame tests to find the metal. Then combine it with the acid radical, or oxide, or hydroxide, to work out the name of the compound.*

ALKALINE → It's alkaline. It's probably an oxide or hydroxide of a metal
- Does it smell of ammonia?
  - **YES →** It's an ammonium compound. Which acid radical does it contain? Do the acid radical tests.
  - **NO →** Do the acid radical tests. If it doesn't contain one of these radicals, it may be an oxide or hydroxide.
- Combine the metal and the acid radical to find the name of the compound.*

NEUTRAL → It's a neutral salt. Which metal does it contain? Do the flame tests.

*The metal always comes first.   **You need a bunsen burner for this experiment.

Computer program

If you have a microcomputer, or can borrow one, you could use it to try out the tests for identifying an unknown substance. This program is written to work on a BBC microcomputer. Lines that need changing for other computers are marked with a symbol and printed at the end of the program. Each symbol corresponds to a different computer. They are:

▲ VIC and PET
■ ZX SPECTRUM
● APPLE
○ ORIC
■ ZX SPECTRUM, DRAGON and TRS-80

```
 10 REM * IDENTIFYING SUBSTANCES *
 20 REM * --------------------- *
 30 GOSUB 930
 40 GOSUB 830
 50 LET N=1
●▲ 60 CLS
 70 REM * MAIN LOOP *
 80 PRINT
 90 PRINT Q$(N);
100 LET F=A(N,1)
110 IF F=0 THEN GOSUB 230
120 IF F=1 THEN GOSUB 310
130 IF N<>0 THEN GOTO 80
140 REM * END PAGE *
150 PRINT
160 PRINT "THATS AS FAR AS WE CAN GO"
170 PRINT "DO YOU WANT TO RUN "
180 PRINT "THE PROGRAM AGAIN? (Y/N)"
190 INPUT A$
200 IF A$="Y" THEN GOTO 40
210 PRINT "O.K "
220 STOP
230 REM * PRINT A STATEMENT *
240 PRINT:PRINT
250 GOSUB 690
260 LET P=A(N,2)
270 IF P=1 THEN GOSUB 360
280 IF P=2 THEN GOSUB 590
290 LET N=A(N,3)
300 RETURN
310 REM * ASK A QUESTION *
320 PRINT " ?":PRINT
330 GOSUB 740
340 LET N=A(N,R+1)
▲● 350 CLS:RETURN
360 REM * FLAME TEST *
▲● 370 CLS:PRINT
380 PRINT "FLAME TESTS"
390 PRINT
400 PRINT "REFER TO PAGE 27 OF"
410 PRINT "THE BOOK FOR THE "
420 PRINT "DETAILS OF THIS TEST"
430 PRINT
440 PRINT "DO YOU HAVE A RESULT?"
450 GOSUB 740
460 IF R=2 THEN GOSUB 480
470 RETURN
480 REM * BORAX TEST *
▲● 490 CLS:PRINT
500 PRINT "BORAX BEAD TEST"
510 PRINT
520 PRINT "REFER TO PAGES 38-39"
530 PRINT "OF THE BOOK FOR THE "
540 PRINT "DETAILS OF THIS TEST"
550 PRINT
560 GOSUB 690
▲● 570 CLS
580 RETURN
590 REM * ACID TEST *
▲● 600 CLS:PRINT
610 PRINT "ACID RADICAL TEST":PRINT
620 PRINT
630 PRINT "REFER TO PAGES 38-39"
640 PRINT "OF THE BOOK FOR THE "
650 PRINT "DETAILS OF THIS TEST"
660 PRINT
670 GOSUB 690
680 RETURN
690 REM * KEY PRESS *
700 PRINT "PRESS SPACE TO CONTINUE"
■▲●○ 710 LET A$=INKEY$(0)
720 IF A$<>" " THEN GOTO 710
730 RETURN
740 REM * GET Y/N ANSWER *
750 PRINT
760 LET R=0
770 PRINT "ANSWER Y/N"
780 INPUT A$
790 IF A$="Y" THEN LET R=1
```

```
800 IF A$="N" THEN LET R=2
810 IF R=0 THEN GOTO 780
820 RETURN
830 REM * INTRO PAGE *
▲●840 CLS:PRINT
850 PRINT "IDENTIFYING SUBSTANCES"
860 PRINT "---------------------"
870 PRINT
880 PRINT "TRY THESE TESTS ON"
890 PRINT "EACH SUBSTANCE."
900 PRINT
910 GOSUB 690
920 CLS:RETURN
930 REM * READ IN THE DATA *
■940 DIM Q$(54),A(54,3)
950 LET K=1
960 READ A$
970 IF A$="END OF DATA" THEN RETURN
980 LET Q$(K)=A$
990 FOR I=1 TO 3
1000 READ A(K,I)
1010 NEXT I
1020 LET K=K+1
1030 GOTO 960
1040 REM * THE DATA *
1050 DATA "DOES IT CONDUCT HEAT OR ELECTRICITY",1,2,5,"IT'S A METAL. IS IT MAGNETIC",1,3,4
1060 DATA "IT IS, OR CONTAINS IRON",0,0,0,"TRY FLAME TESTS",0,1,0
1070 DATA "DOES IT MELT EASILY",1,6,17,"IT'S A COVALENT COMPOUND OR ELEMENT",0,0,7
1080 DATA "IS IT A YELLOW POWDER",1,10,8,"OR A RED/YELLOW SOLID",1,11,9
1090 DATA "OR A PURPLE/BLACK SOLID",1,12,13,"IT'S PROBABLY SULPHUR",0,0,0
1100 DATA "IT'S PROBABLY PHOSPHOROUS",0,0,0,"IT'S PROBABLY IODINE",0,0,0
1110 DATA "IT COULD BE AN ORGANIC COMPOUND",0,0,14,"HEAT IT. IS CARBON DIOXIDE GIVEN OFF",1,16,15
1120 DATA "IT'S NOT ORGANIC",0,0,0,"IT'S ORGANIC AND CONTAINS CARBON",0,0,0
1130 DATA "IT'S PROBABLY AN IONIC COMPOUND",0,0,18,"DOES IT DISSOLVE",1,24,19
1140 DATA "IS IT A BLACK POWDER",1,20,23,"HEAT IT. IS CARBON DIOXIDE GIVEN OFF",1,21,22
1150 DATA "IT'S CARBON",0,0,0,"IT'S COPPER OXIDE",0,0,0
1160 DATA "IT'S AN INSOLUBLE SALT",0,0,29,"FIND PH RATING",0,0,25
1170 DATA "IS IT AN ACID",1,42,26,"IS IT AN ALKALI",1,33,27
1180 DATA "IS IT NEUTRAL",1,28,25,"IT'S A NEUTRAL SALT",0,0,29
1190 DATA "FIND METAL CONTAINED",0,1,30,"FIND THE ACID CONTAINED",0,2,31
1200 DATA "COMBINE THE METAL AND THE ACID RADICAL",0,0,32,"TO FIND THE COMPOUND NAME",0,0,0
1210 DATA "IT COULD BE AN OXIDE OR...",0,0,34,"HYDROXIDE OF A METAL",0,0,35
1220 DATA "DOES IT SMELL OF AMMONIA",1,54,36,"DO ACID RADICAL TEST",0,2,37
1230 DATA "DO YOU HAVE A RESULT",1,39,38,"IT'S PROBABLY AN OXIDE OR HYDROXIDE",0,0,39
1240 DATA "FIND THE METAL CONTAINED",0,1,40,"COMBINE WITH THE ACID RADICAL",0,0,41
1250 DATA "OR OXIDE OR HYDROXIDE FOR COMPOUND",0,0,0,"ADD ZINC. IS HYDROGEN GIVEN OFF",1,44,43
1260 DATA "IT'S AN ACID SALT",0,0,29,"IT'S AN ACID",0,0,45
1270 DATA "DO ACID RADICAL TEST",0,2,46,"IS THE RADICAL SULPHATE",1,49,47
1280 DATA "OR CHLORIDE",1,50,48,"OR CARBONATE",1,51,52
1290 DATA "IT'S SULPHURIC ACID",0,0,0,"IT'S HYDROCHLORIC ACID",0,0,0
1300 DATA "IT'S CARBONIC ACID",0,0,0,"IT COULD BE A NITRATE OR...",0,0,53
1310 DATA "BROMIDE OR IODIDE",0,0,0,"IT'S AN AMMONIUM COMPOUND",0,0,0
1320 DATA "END OF DATA"
```

Below is a list of changes that will enable you to run this program on other computers too. These instructions need to be inserted into the program in the relevant places.

■ 710 LET A$=INKEY$
▲ 710 GET A$
● 705 A$=""
● 710 IF PEEK-16384>127 THEN GET A$
○ 710 LET A$=KEY$
● 60,350,370,490,570,600,840 HOME
▲ 60,350,370,490,570,600,840 PRINT CHR$(147)
■ 940 DIM Q$(54,38):DIM A(54,3)

Formulae and equations

The chemical formula of a substance shows what elements it contains and in what proportions. In a covalent compound, it tells you the exact numbers of atoms of each element in a molecule of the substance.

What the symbols mean

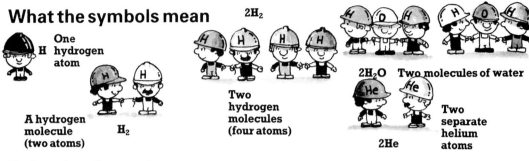

One H hydrogen atom

A hydrogen molecule (two atoms) H_2

$2H_2$ Two hydrogen molecules (four atoms)

$2H_2O$ Two molecules of water

$2He$ Two separate helium atoms

Balancing formulae

You may have read about how to work out formulae from valencies on page 21. Here are a few more points to remember.

Radicals, such as carbonate, have a single valency, even though they are made up of more than one element. If you have to multiply a radical, you show this in the formula by putting the number after a pair of brackets. For example, magnesium has a valency of two and nitrate has a valency of one. The formula for magnesium nitrate is $Mg(NO_3)_2$, which shows that there is one magnesium and two nitrates.

Now try working out the formula of sodium carbonate and magnesium hydroxide. Valencies: sodium (Na) 1, magnesium (Mg) 2, carbonate (CO_3) 2, hydroxide (OH) 1.

With an ionic compound, it is important to consider the charge on the ion, as well as its valency. An ionic compound is electrically neutral, so the charges must cancel each other out. There must be as many positives as negatives. Sodium and potassium both have valencies of one, but they cannot combine because their ions both have positive charges. However sodium will combine with chlorine which has a valency of one, because a chloride ion has a negative charge.

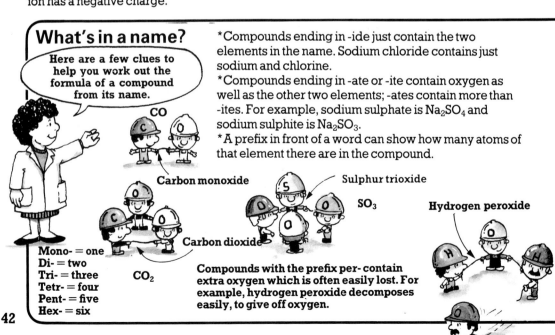

What's in a name?

Here are a few clues to help you work out the formula of a compound from its name.

*Compounds ending in -ide just contain the two elements in the name. Sodium chloride contains just sodium and chlorine.
*Compounds ending in -ate or -ite contain oxygen as well as the other two elements; -ates contain more than -ites. For example, sodium sulphate is Na_2SO_4 and sodium sulphite is Na_2SO_3.
*A prefix in front of a word can show how many atoms of that element there are in the compound.

CO Carbon monoxide

CO_2 Carbon dioxide

Sulphur trioxide SO_3

Hydrogen peroxide

Mono- = one
Di- = two
Tri- = three
Tetr- = four
Pent- = five
Hex- = six

Compounds with the prefix per- contain extra oxygen which is often easily lost. For example, hydrogen peroxide decomposes easily, to give off oxygen.

Equations

Equations are a way of writing down chemical reactions in a sort of shorthand. In an equation, the formulae are used instead of the names of the chemicals. Here are some of the signs and symbols you may see in an equation.

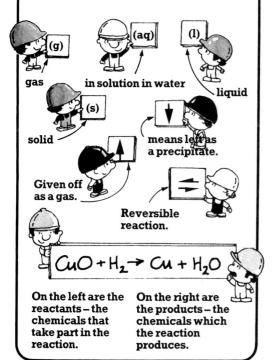

On the left are the reactants – the chemicals that take part in the reaction.

On the right are the products – the chemicals which the reaction produces.

Balancing equations

A basic law of chemistry* states that you cannot create or destroy matter in a chemical reaction. Although the chemicals change their form, the same number of atoms remain. The products of a reaction may appear to be lighter than the reactants if one of the products is given off as a gas. When you write equations, you have to show that atoms are not made or destroyed. So the number of atoms on one side of an equation must be the same as on the other.

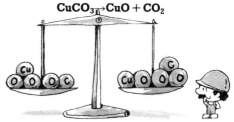

For example, look at this equation showing copper carbonate decomposing to form copper oxide and carbon dioxide. Count up the atoms and you will see that the equation balances. On each side there are three oxygens, one copper and one carbon.

Many equations are more difficult than this one. This equation for making water doesn't balance, because there is one less oxygen on the right. You can't write $H_2 + O \rightarrow H_2O$, because oxygen doesn't exist as O. The atoms always go around in pairs. Water contains twice as much hydrogen as oxygen, so try the equation with two molecules of hydrogen to one of oxygen.

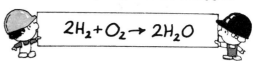

If you count up the atoms, you will see that the equation is balanced. There are four hydrogens and two oxygens on each side. This shows that no atoms have been created or destroyed in the reaction.

The new naming system

These days chemists are using a new system for naming compounds. It involves including the combining power of the element in the name. For example, MnO_2 is often called manganese dioxide, but it is also called manganese IV oxide. (You may have used it as a catalyst on page 24.) MnO_2 is an ionic compound. Each oxygen ion has two negative charges, which together make four. When a manganese ion combines with two oxygen ions, it must have four positive charges, in order to cancel them out. This is why it is called manganese IV oxide. In other compounds, manganese can have a different valency or combining power.

*This is called the law of conservation of mass.

Doing experiments

A lot of things can affect your experiments, with unexpected results. Always keep your equipment clean and dry, as dirt and traces of other chemicals can interfere with the reaction. The temperature of the room can be important too. It could be speeding up or slowing down your experiment.

With a lot of experiments, it is important to do a "control". A control is an experiment which exactly copies the experiment you are doing, except for one important factor or ingredient. For example, if you do an experiment to show the effect of a catalyst, you should also do the same experiment without the catalyst. This shows you that the catalyst is having an effect, and that the same reaction would not have happened anyway – or at least not at the same speed.

Always weigh or measure your chemicals as accurately as possible. The quantities and concentration of chemicals used can affect the reaction too. Finally, being a good scientist involves keeping detailed notes on the results of your experiments. This can help you build on what you already know, without having to do the same experiments all over again.

Equipment and chemicals

There are a lot of experiments you can do without a proper chemistry set. You can probably find most of the equipment you need around the house, and some of the chemicals too. Here are some ideas for getting hold of chemicals and equipment you may need.

Jam jars can be used instead of test tubes. It's best to use glass containers for experiments. They are easier to see through than plastic.

As a funnel, you could chop off the top of a bottle of washing up liquid.

Droppers are useful. You can find these on old bottles of eye, ear or nose drops.

As filter paper, you could use coffee filters or blotting paper. (Kitchen towel doesn't work as well.)

Tin foil is made from aluminium. You can use this for electrodes.

Pencil leads can be used instead of carbon electrodes in many experiments.

Nichrome wire comes from electrical shops. Heat the end gently and press it into a cork. Then you can use the cork as a handle.

Batteries, small bulbs, thermometers and magnets will be useful for various experiments. You could use a candle to heat things, if you haven't got a spirit burner.

A measuring jug is useful too. You could borrow one or make your own from a jam jar. Fill the jug with water to the first measure. Pour it into your jar and make a mark on the side. You could use masking tape to write on. Then do the same for all the other measures.

You may be able to borrow some kitchen scales for weighing things. Use a piece of polythene or something to keep it clean.

You can buy rubber or plastic tubing at wine-making stores.

For iron, use wire wool or nails.

To get copper, strip the plastic from electrical wire.

Vinegar can be used as an acid in many experiments.

Crushed eggshell, marble, limestone and chalk (from chalk cliffs) are all forms of calcium carbonate.

You can buy a lot of chemicals at the chemist, such as iodine, sulphur and litmus papers.

Safety notes

★ Always take great care when handling chemicals. Mop up all spills and wash your hands thoroughly after experiments. Never taste chemicals, or eat while you are doing experiments. Keep your hands away from your eyes. Some chemists wear goggles to protect their eyes.

★ Follow the instructions for experiments carefully. Keep all your chemicals labelled and out of the reach of young children.

★ It is a good idea to keep equipment that you use for experiments separate from other household equipment.

★ Be especially careful with heat and electricity. Don't touch red hot test tubes, without using special heatproof tongs.

Answers

Page 9
A saucepan overflows when it is boiling because particles of gas take up more space than the same number of particles of liquid. As a liquid boils, it changes into a gas. When this happen, the amount of space it takes up increases.

Page 10: Separating puzzle
To separate tea and sugar, dissolve them in cold water and then filter the solution. The tea does not dissolve, so it is filtered off. To get back the sugar, boil or evaporate the solution. You can use the same method to separate salt and flour, or a broken bottle of bath salts. To separate talc and bath salts, you could just add water. The talc does not dissolve and should float on the surface. To separate a broken jar of pins, use a magnet.

Page 17: Atom puzzle
An atom of potassium or sodium will react with one atom or chlorine, bromine or iodine. An atom of magnesium or calcium will react with an atom of sulphur. A helium atom will not normally react at all. When larger numbers of atoms are involved, all of these atoms are able to react together, except helium.

Page 20: Compound puzzle
Sugar, methylated spirits and bicycle oil are all covalent compounds. Epsom salts is an ionic compound.

Page 24
Chemists keep hydrogen peroxide in dark bottles, to stop it reacting with light and decomposing.

Page 27
Nothing can burn on the Moon because there is no oxygen there. Burning is a reaction involving oxygen.

Page 28
Apple juice is acidic. Toothpaste and ammonia are alkaline. Paraffin and sugar are neutral. Salt is normally neutral too, but the salt we eat contains additives which make it slightly alkaline.

Page 33.
Dimethyl ether is an isomer of ethanol. Its structure looks like this:

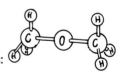

Page 37
There are more bubbles at the positive electrode than at the negative one because the positive electrode attracts hydrogen. Water contains twice as much hydrogen as oxygen.

If sodium carbonate and zinc sulphate are dissolved together, zinc carbonate will be the precipitate.

Page 42
Sodium carbonate is Na_2CO_3.
Magnesium hydroxide is $Mg(OH)_2$.

Chemistry words

Acid. A substance which contains hydrogen that can be replaced by a metal. In solution, it turns litmus red.
Activation energy. The energy needed to start a reaction.
Alkali. A substance which will neutralize an acid to produce a salt and water only. It turns litmus blue. A soluble base.
Anion. An ion with a negative electric charge. An atom which has gained one or more electrons.
Anode. A positive electrode. Electrode which discharges electrons.
Atom. The smallest particle of an element which can exist and still retain the properties of that element.
Atomic number. The number of electrons or protons of an atom of a particular element.
Base. The hydroxide or oxide of a metal. A substance which reacts with an acid to form a salt and water only. It does not dissolve.
Catalyst. A substance which alters the speed of a reaction, but remains unchanged itself at the end of the reaction.
Cathode. A negative electrode.
Cation. An ion with a positive electric charge. An atom which has lost one or more electrons.
Combustion. Burning. Oxidation which gives out heat and light (flame).
Compound. A substance containing two or more elements which have been chemically combined.
Covalent compound. A compound made up of atoms of different elements sharing pairs of electrons.
Decomposition. The process of breaking down a substance into a simpler one. For example, splitting a compound into its elements.
Electrode. A conductor by which an electric current enters or leaves during electrolysis.
Electrolysis. The decomposition of a substance, when melted or in solution, by passing an electric current through it.
Electrolyte. A substance which allows electricity to pass through it.
Electron. A negatively charged particle in an atom.
Element. A substance which cannot be split chemically into a simpler substance. A chemical whose atoms all have the same number of protons.
Equation. The way chemists write down chemical reactions, using the symbols and formulae of the chemicals taking part.
Formula. A way of describing the composition of a substance, using symbols and numbers.
Ion. A charged particle; an atom or group of atoms which has lost or gained electrons.
Ionic compound. A compound made up of ions.
Isotope. Atoms of an element which have different mass numbers are different isotopes of that element.
Lattice. A structure in which atoms, or ions, are tightly bonded together, in a regular or rigid pattern.
Mass number. The sum of protons and neutrons in the nucleus of an atom of a particular element.
Molecule. The smallest particle of a substance which can normally exist by itself and still have the properties of that substance.
Neutralization. The removal of acidity or alkalinity in a substance; the reaction between an acid and an alkali to form a salt and water.
Neutron. A neutral, uncharged particle in the nucleus of an atom.
Oxidation. The reaction between a substance and oxygen, to form an oxide. It can also mean the removal of hydrogen or the loss of electrons.
pH scale. The measure of acidity or alkalinity in a substance.
Precipitate. A solid which forms and settles in a solution.
Products. The substances formed as a result of a chemical change.
Proton. A positively charged particle in the nucleus of an atom.
Radical. A group of elements bonded together, which behave chemically as a single atom.
Reduction. The opposite of oxidation; the removal of oxygen, the addition of hydrogen or the gain of electrons.
Relative atomic mass. The mass of an atom relative to the mass of an atom of carbon 12, which is said to have a mass of 12. The relative atomic mass of an element

is the average mass of all the different isotopes of that element.
Salt. An ionic compound, formed when the hydrogen of an acid is replaced by a metal.
Solubility. The extent to which a substance will dissolve.
Solution. A soluble solid dissolved in a liquid.
Solvent. The medium in which a substance is dissolved.
Suspension. An insoluble solid suspended in a liquid; a liquid containing a substance which will not dissolve.
Valency. The combining power of an element; a number indicating the number of electrons gained, lost or shared in chemical bonding.

Useful information
Alphabetical list of elements

Ac	Actinium	Er	Erbium	Mn	Manganese	Sm	Samarium
Al	Aluminium	Eu	Europium	Md	Mendelevium	Sc	Scandium
Am	Americium	Fm	Fermium	Hg	Mercury	Se	Selenium
Sb	Antimony	F	Fluorine	Mo	Molybdenum	Si	Silicon
Ar	Argon	Fr	Francium	Nd	Neodymium	Ag	Silver
As	Arsenic	Gd	Gadolinium	Ne	Neon	Na	Sodium
At	Astatine	Ga	Gallium	Np	Neptunium	Sr	Strontium
Ba	Barium	Ge	Germanium	Ni	Nickel	S	Sulphur
Bk	Berkelium	Au	Gold	Nb	Niobium	Ta	Tantalum
Be	Beryllium	Hf	Hafnium	Os	Osmium	Tc	Technetium
Bi	Bismuth	Ha	Hahnium	O	Oxygen	Te	Tellerium
B	Boron	He	Helium	Pd	Palladium	Tb	Terbium
Br	Bromine	Ho	Holmium	P	Phosphorus	Tl	Thallium
Cd	Cadmium	H	Hydrogen	Pt	Platinum	Th	Thorium
Cs	Caesium	In	Indium	Pu	Plutonium	Tm	Thulium
Ca	Calcium	I	Iodine	Po	Polonium	Sn	Tin
Cf	Californium	Ir	Iridium	K	Potassium	Ti	Titanium
C	Carbon	Fe	Iron	Pr	Praseodymium	W	Tungsten
Ce	Cerium	Kr	Krypton	Pm	Promethium	U	Uranium
Cl	Clorine	Ku	Kurtschatovium	Pa	Protoactinium	V	Vanadium
Cr	Chromium	La	Lanthanum	Ra	Radium	Xe	Xenon
Co	Cobalt	Lr	Lawrencium	Rn	Radon	Yb	Ytterbium
Cu	Copper	Pb	Lead	Re	Rhenium	Y	Yttium
Cm	Curium	Li	Lithium	Rh	Rhodium	Zn	Zinc
Dy	Dysprosium	Lu	Lutetium	Rb	Rubidium	Zr	Zirconium
Es	Einsteinium	Mg	Magnesium	Ru	Ruthenium		

Valencies of some important elements

Aluminium	3	Copper	1,2	Nitrogen	3,5
Arsenic	3,5	Fluorine	1	Oxygen	2
Barium	2	Gold	1	Phosphorus	3,5
Bromine	1	Hydrogen	1	Potassium	1
Cadmium	2	Iodine	1	Rhubidium	1
Caesium	1	Iron	2,3	Silicon	4
Calcium	2	Lead	2,4	Silver	1
Carbon	4	Lithium	1	Strontium	2
Chlorine	1,7	Magnesium	2	Sulphur	2,4,6
Chromium	3,6	Mercury	1,2	Tin	2,4
Cobalt	2,3	Nickel	2	Zinc	2

Activity series of metals

Potassium	**most reactive**
Sodium	
Calcium	
Magnesium	
Aluminium	
Zinc	Copper
Iron	Mercury
Tin	Silver
Lead	Gold
Hydrogen	**least reactive**

Index

acids, 28-29
acid radical tests, 39
acid rain, 22
acropolis, Athens, 22
actinide metals, 14
activation energy, 25
activity series, 26, 29
alchemy, 4
alcohol, 31
   manufacture of, 11
alkali, 28, 29
alkanes, 32, 34
alkenes, 33
alkynes, 33
aluminium, 26
amino acid, 31
ammonia, 21
amylase, 30
anode, 19
argon, 16
atom, 4, 6, 7, 8, 10, 12, 16, 20, 21, 30, 32
atomic mass, relative, 6, 15, 46
atomic number, 6, 15
atomic weight, 14

bases, 28-29
bee stings, 29
borax bead test, 39
Boyle, Robert, 4
burning, 27
butane, 32

carbohydrates, 13, 30, 31
carbon, 6, 15, 20, 21, 30, 32
carbon 14, 7
carbon dioxide, 8, 12, 21, 22, 29, 30, 31, 42
   testing for, 30
catalyst, 24-25, 30-31, 44
cathode, 19
changes of state, 8, 9
chemical bonding, 12, 18, 19, 20
chlorine, 12, 17, 21, 42
chromatography, 11
combustion, 26
compound, 10, 12-13, 18-19, 21, 26, 27, 28, 30, 32, 36, 37, 42
condensing, 9
control experiment, 44
copper, 6, 26, 27
covalent compounds, 20, 21, 43
cracking, 34
Crick, Francis, 31
crude oil, 34
cyclic hydrocarbons, 33

Dalton, John, 4
decomposition, 24, 36
density, 5
digestion, 30-31
displacement reaction, 27
distillation, 11
DNA (deoxyribonucleic acid), 31
Döbereiner, 14
double bond, 33, 35
double decomposition, 36

electricity, 18, 19, 37
electrodes, 18, 19, 37, 46
electrolysis, 37, 46
electrolyte, 37
electron, 6, 7, 16, 17, 19, 20, 21, 46
elements, 3, 6, 10, 14, 15, 20, 21, 37, 46
enzyme, 25, 30, 31
equations, 42-43
ethanoic acid, 31
esters, 35
ethanol, 31, 32, 33
ethene, 33
evaporating, 9, 10, 11

fats, 30, 31, 35
fermentation, 31
fireworks, 27
flame tests, 27, 38
formulae, 4, 21, 42-43
fractional distillation, 34
freezing, 9
fridge, 8

galvanise, 26
glucose, 30
groups, of elements, 14-15

halogens, 15, 17
heat energy, 9, 12, 23, 27
helium, 16, 17
hydrangeas, 29
hydrocarbons, 32, 33, 35
hydrogen, 8, 14, 20, 21, 28, 30, 32
   testing for, 29
hydroxide, 28, 42

indigestion, 29
inert gases, 15, 16
ion, 19, 20, 28, 36, 37, 46
ionic compounds, 19
isomers, 32, 33
isotope, 7, 14

Kekulé, 33
krypton, 16

lattice, 8, 20, 46
law of conservation of mass, 43
light energy, 13
lipase, 31
litmus paper, 28, 29

margarine, 35
mass number, 7, 46
melting, 9
Mendeleev, Dmitri, 14
metalloid, 14-15
metals, 5, 10, 14, 19, 26, 27
methane, 20, 21, 32
methylpropane, 32
mixtures, 10-11
molecular models, 32
molecule, 8, 10, 12, 20, 30, 33, 34, 46
monomers, 33

negative ions (anions), 19, 37
neon, 16
neutralization, 29

neutron, 7
Newlands, John, 14
non-metals, 5, 10, 14, 19
nuclear power, 7
nucleus, 6, 7

octane rating, 34
orbits, of atoms, 16, 17, 20
organic chemistry, 30-31, 32-33, 34-35
oxidation, 26, 27
oxide, 26, 28
oxygen, 8, 13, 15, 21, 24, 30
   testing for, 24

particle, 6, 7, 8, 9
pepsin, 31
Periodic Table, 14-15, 17, 19
petrol, 34
pH numbers, 28, 46
physical changes, 10
plastics, 34
pollution, 22
polyethene (polythene), 33
polymerization, 33
polymers, 33, 34
polyunsaturates, 35
positive ions (cations), 19, 37
precipitate, 36
proteins, 30, 31
protons, 7

radicals, 28, 42
radioactive isotope, 7
radioactivity, 7
radon, 16
rare earth metals, 14
reduction, 27
relative atomic mass, 6, 14
replacement reaction, 27, 36
rust, 26

salt, table, 11, 12, 17, 29
salts, 28-29, 35, 36
soap, 35
sodium, 12, 17, 19, 26, 27, 42
solution, 10, 47
starch, 25, 30
   test for, 25
subliming, 9
surface tension, 35
suspension, 10, 47

thermoplastics, 34
thermosets, 34
transition metals, 14-15
triple bond, 33

universal indicator, 28

valency, 21, 42

water, 8, 12, 20, 21, 35
   splitting, 37
Watson, James, 31
wine, making, 31

xenon, 16

yeast, 31

zinc, 26, 29

48